Spring
Cakes

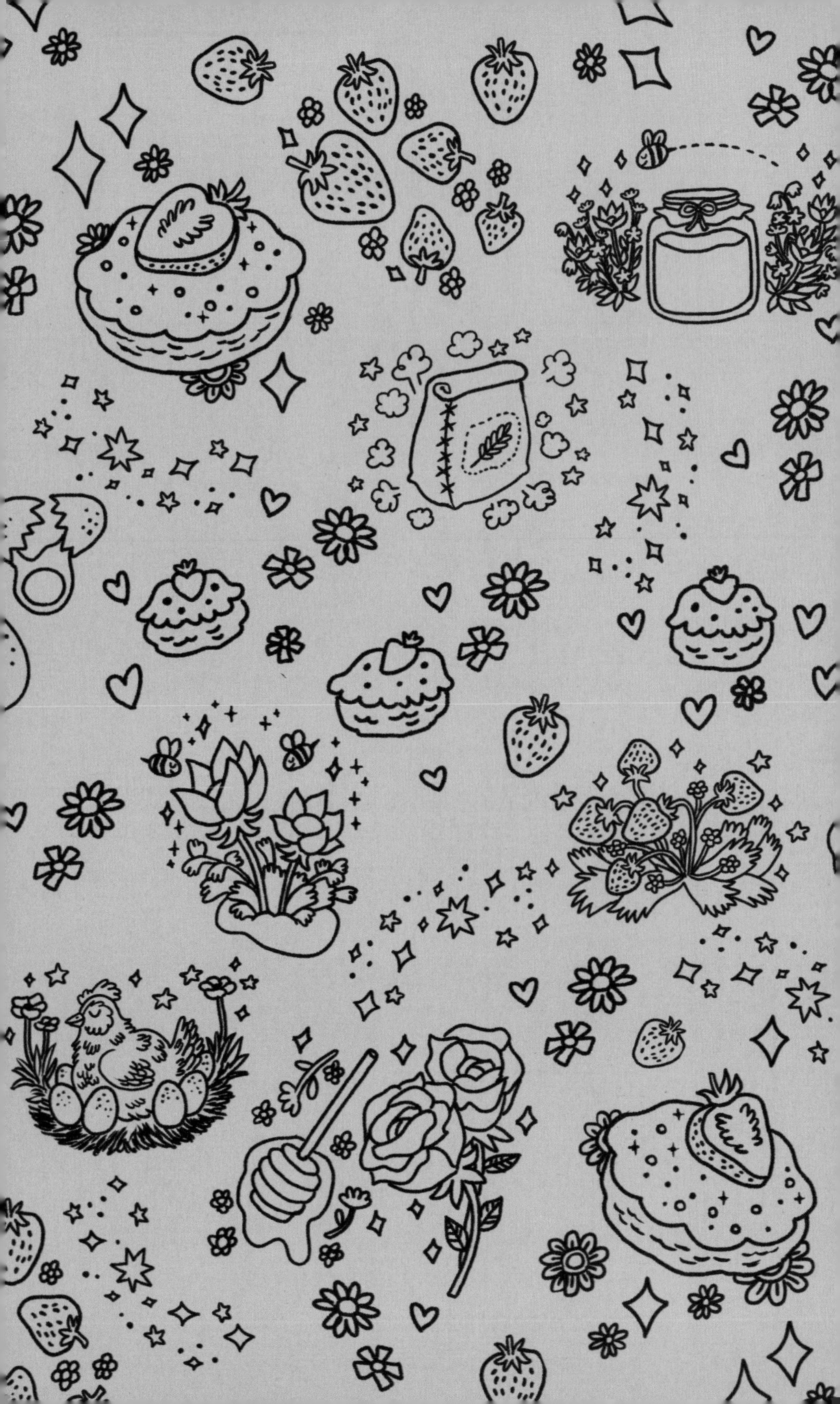

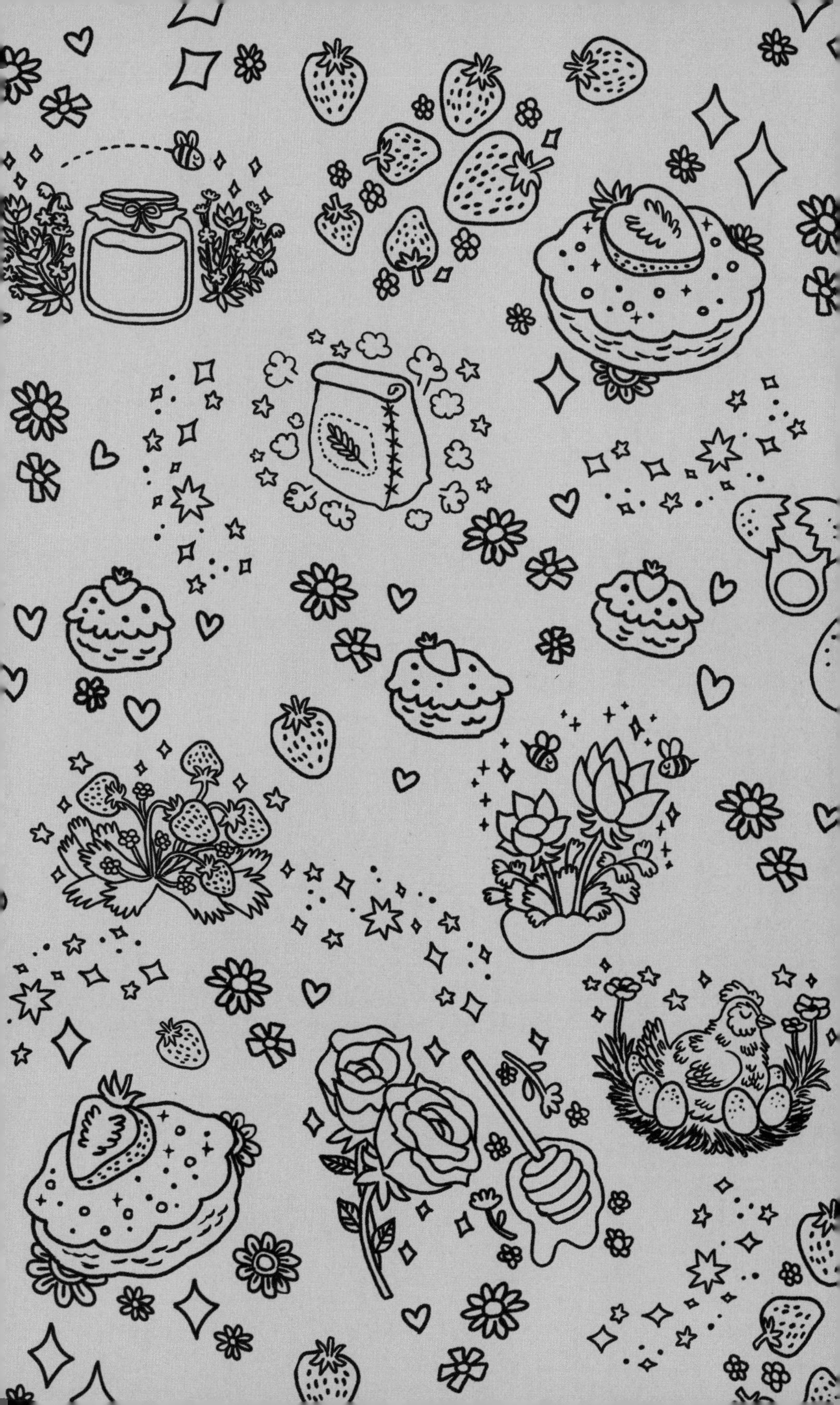

I LIKE TO READ is a registered trademark of Holiday House Publishing, Inc.
Copyright © 2021 by Miranda Harmon
All Rights Reserved
HOLIDAY HOUSE is registered in the U.S. Patent and Trademark Office.
Printed and bound in April 2021 at Leo Paper, Heshan, China.
The artwork was created digitally.
www.holidayhouse.com
3 5 7 9 10 8 6 4 2

Library of Congress Cataloging-in-Publication Data

Names: Harmon, Miranda, author, illustrator.
Title: Spring cakes / Miranda Harmon.
Description: First edition. | New York : Holiday House, 2021. | Series:
I like to read comics | Audience: Ages 4–8. | Audience: Grades K–1.
Summary: "Three kittens, Nutmeg, Cinnamon, and Ginger, go on a quest to
find the magical ingredients to make Mama Cat's famous cupcakes"—
Provided by publisher.
Identifiers: LCCN 2020031470 | ISBN 9780823447534 (hardcover)
Subjects: CYAC: Graphic novels. | Brothers and sisters—Fiction.
Cats—Fiction. | Animals—Infancy—Fiction. | Baking—Fiction.
Magic—Fiction.
Classification: LCC PZ7.7.H3657 Spr 2021 | DDC 741.5/973—dc23
LC record available at https://lccn.loc.gov/2020031470

ISBN: 978-0-8234-4753-4 (Hardcover)
ISBN: 978-0-8234-4935-4 (Paperback)

Spring Cakes

Miranda Harmon

HOLIDAY HOUSE · NEW YORK

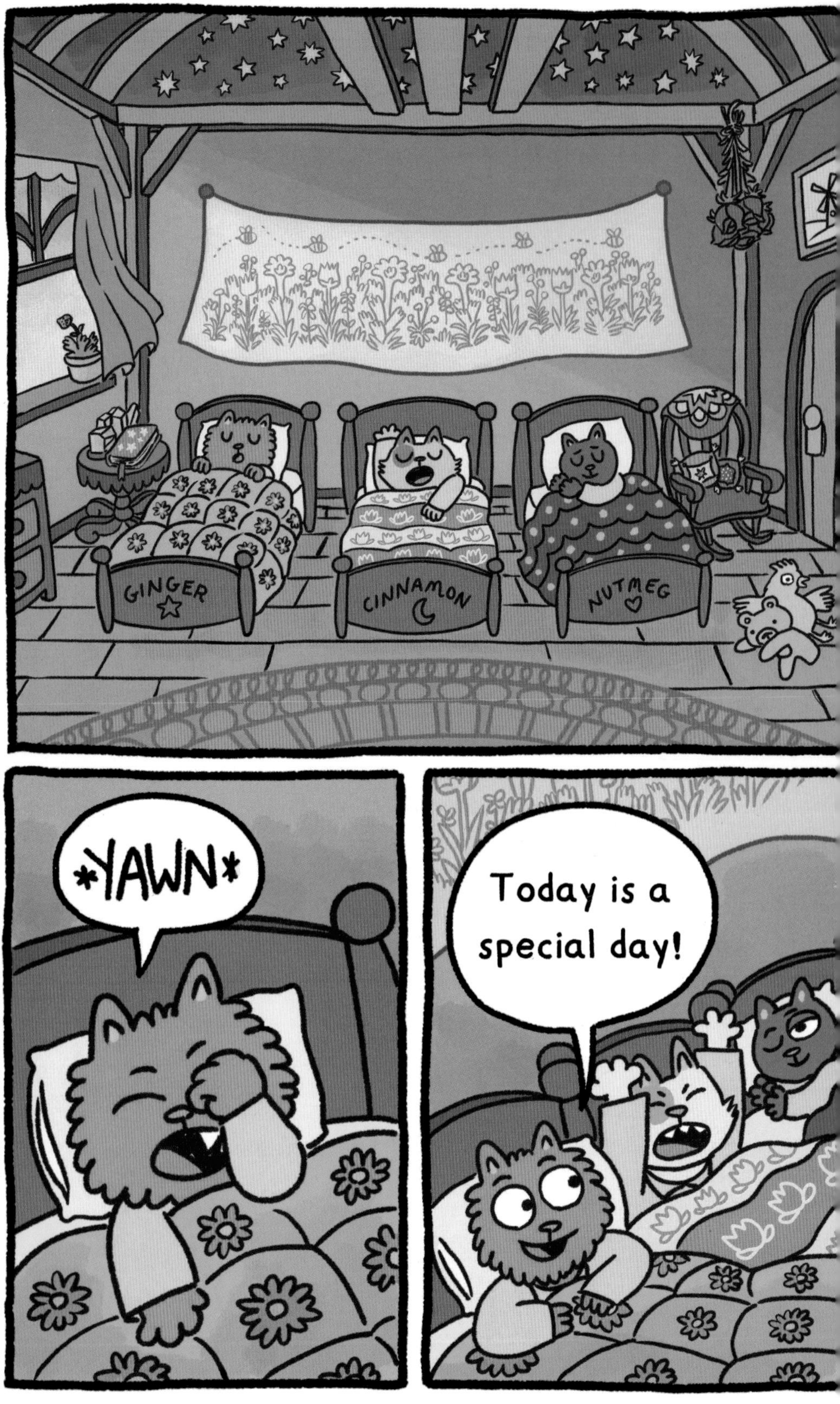
GINGER
CINNAMON
NUTMEG
YAWN
Today is a special day!

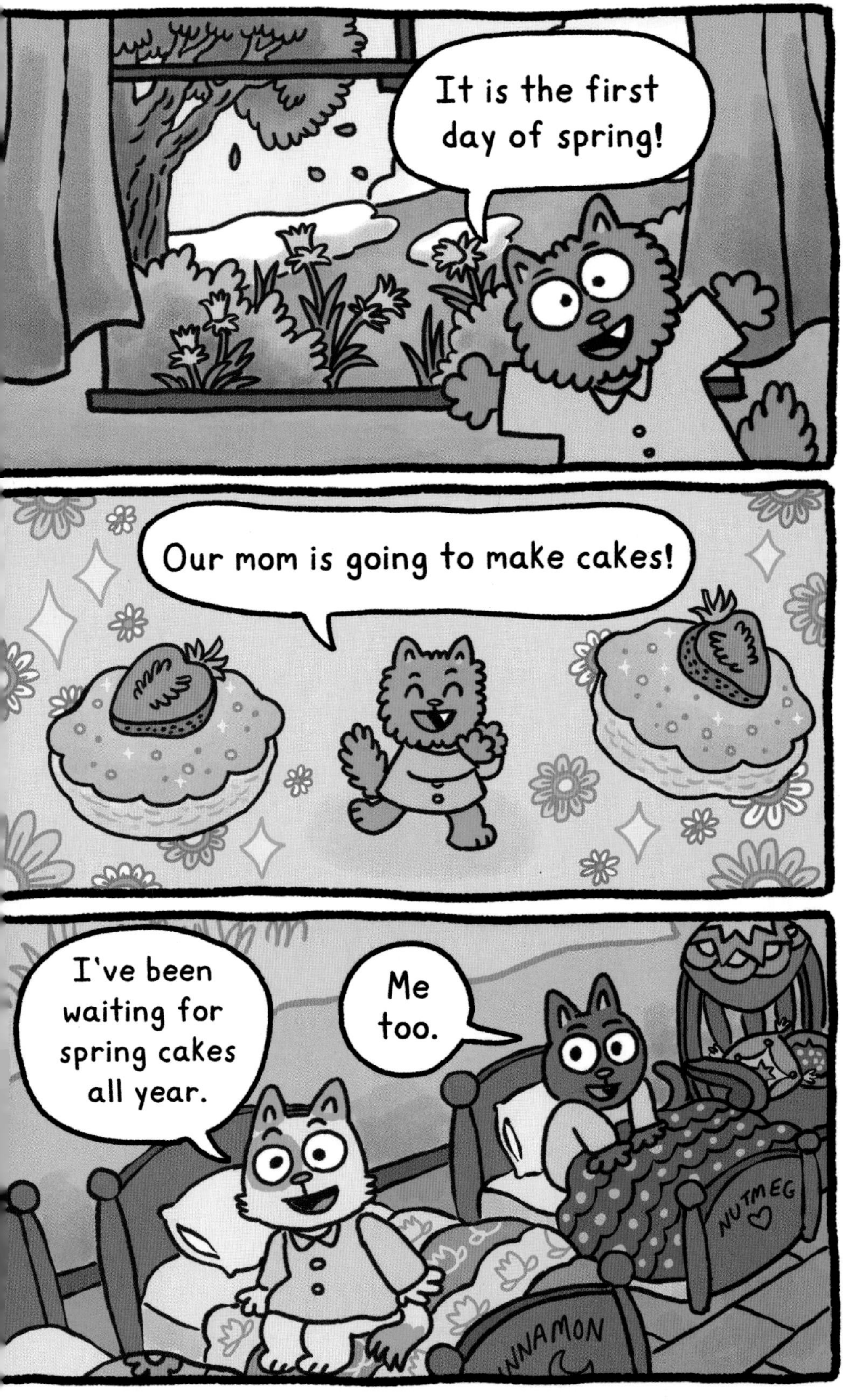
It is the first day of spring!
Our mom is going to make cakes!
I've been waiting for spring cakes all year.
Me too.
NUTMEG
NNAMON

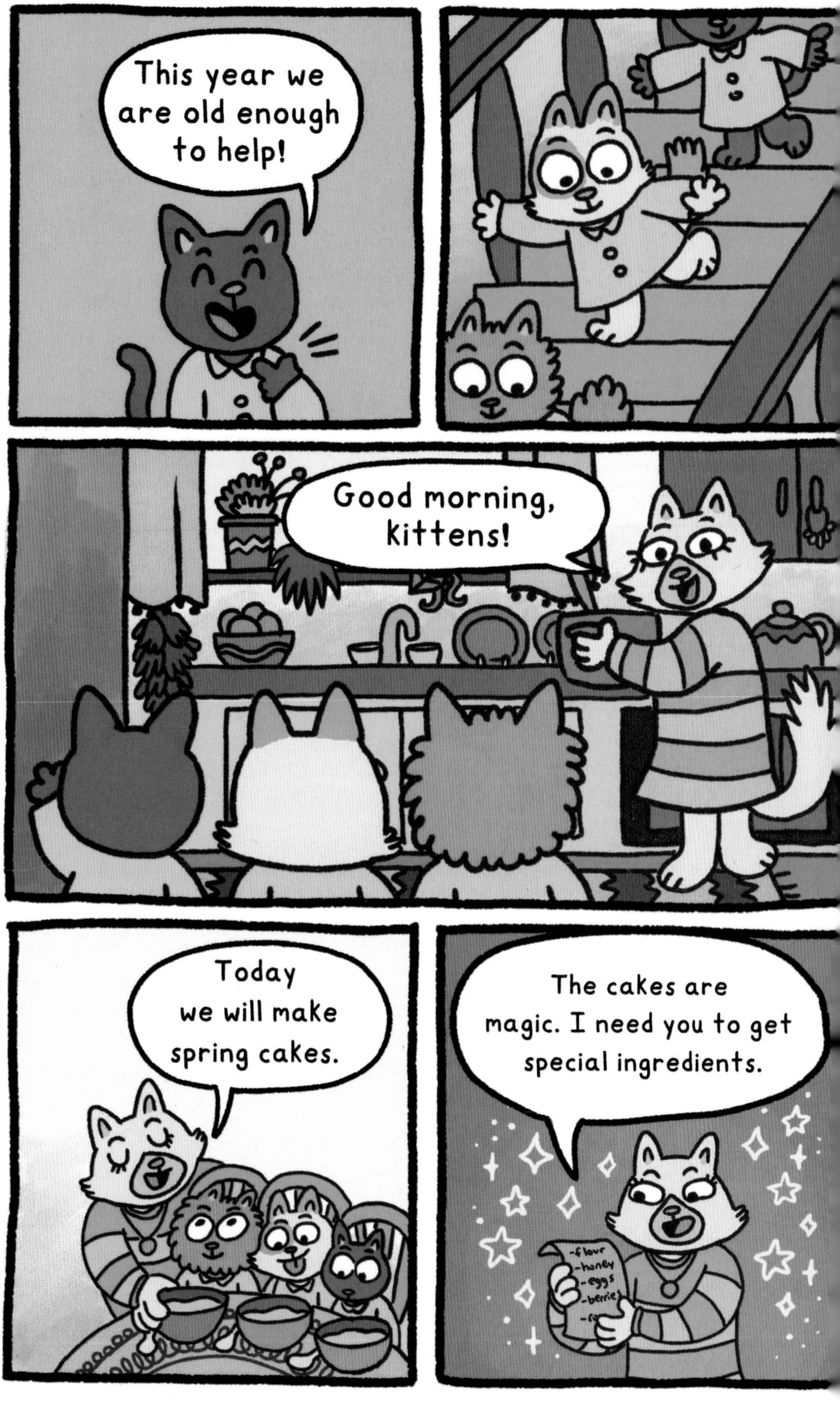
This year we are old enough to help!
Good morning, kittens!
Today we will make spring cakes.
The cakes are magic. I need you to get special ingredients.
-flour
-honey
-eggs

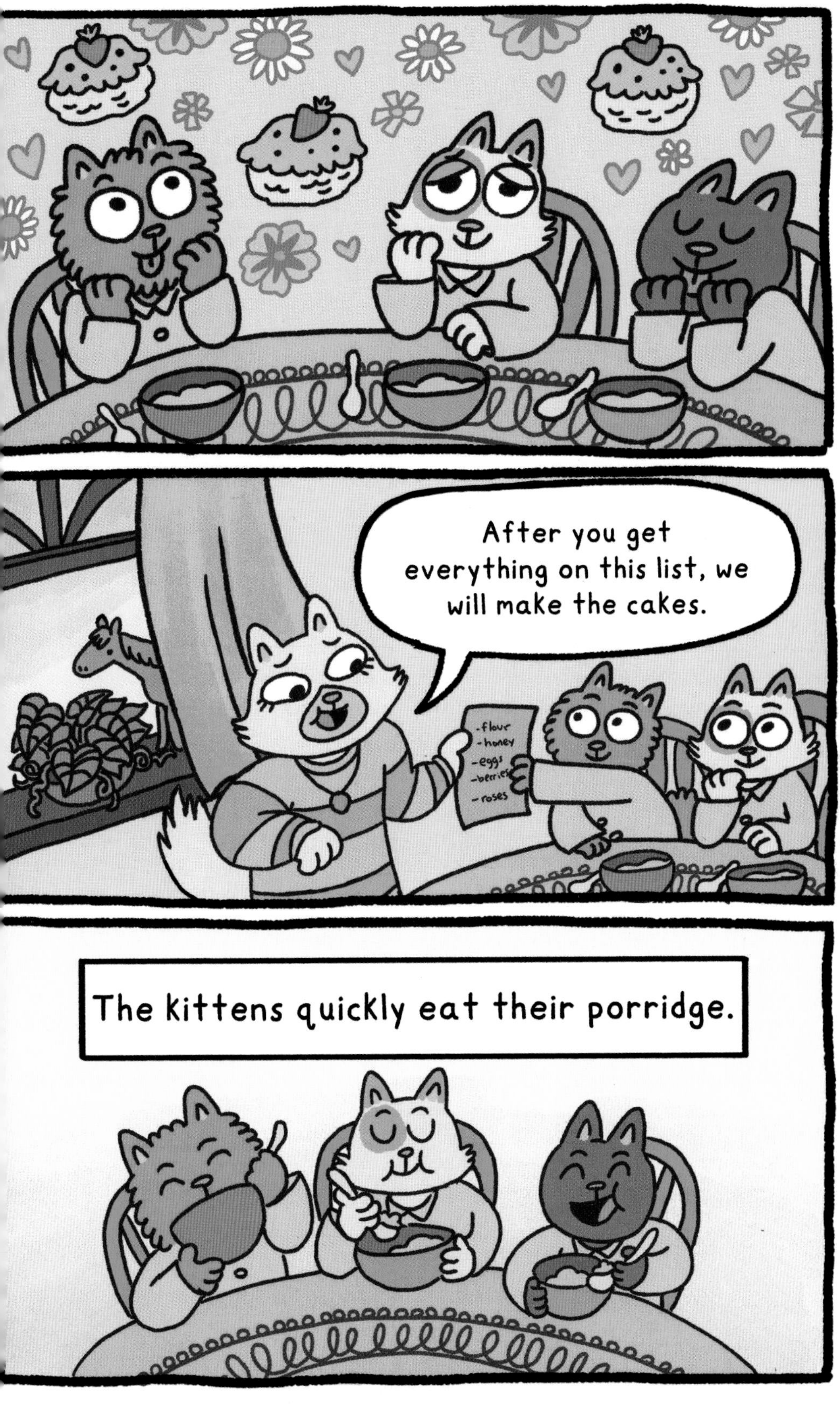
After you get everything on this list, we will make the cakes.
-flour
-honey
-eggs
-berries
-roses
The kittens quickly eat their porridge.

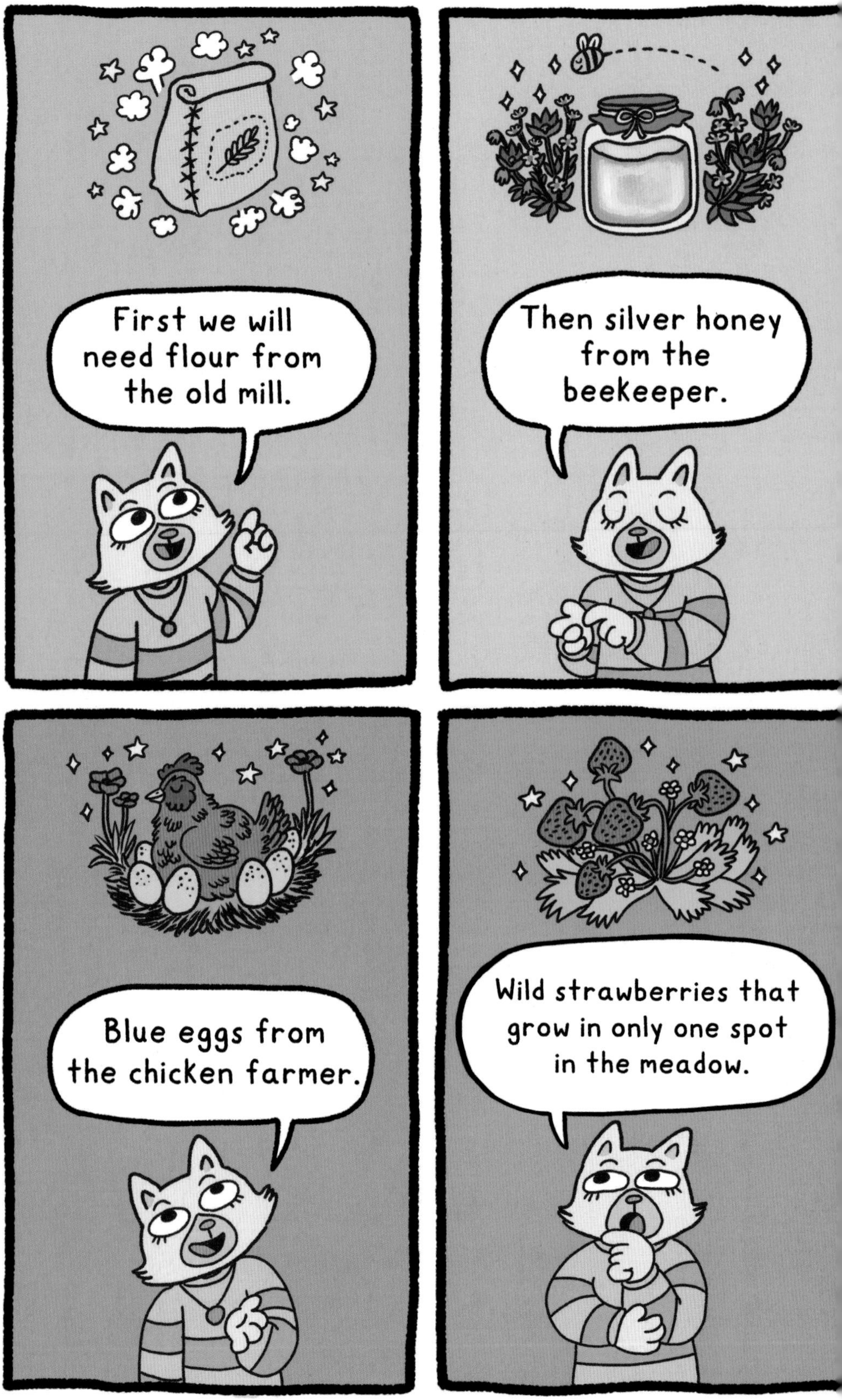
First we will need flour from the old mill.
Then silver honey from the beekeeper.
Blue eggs from the chicken farmer.
Wild strawberries that grow in only one spot in the meadow.

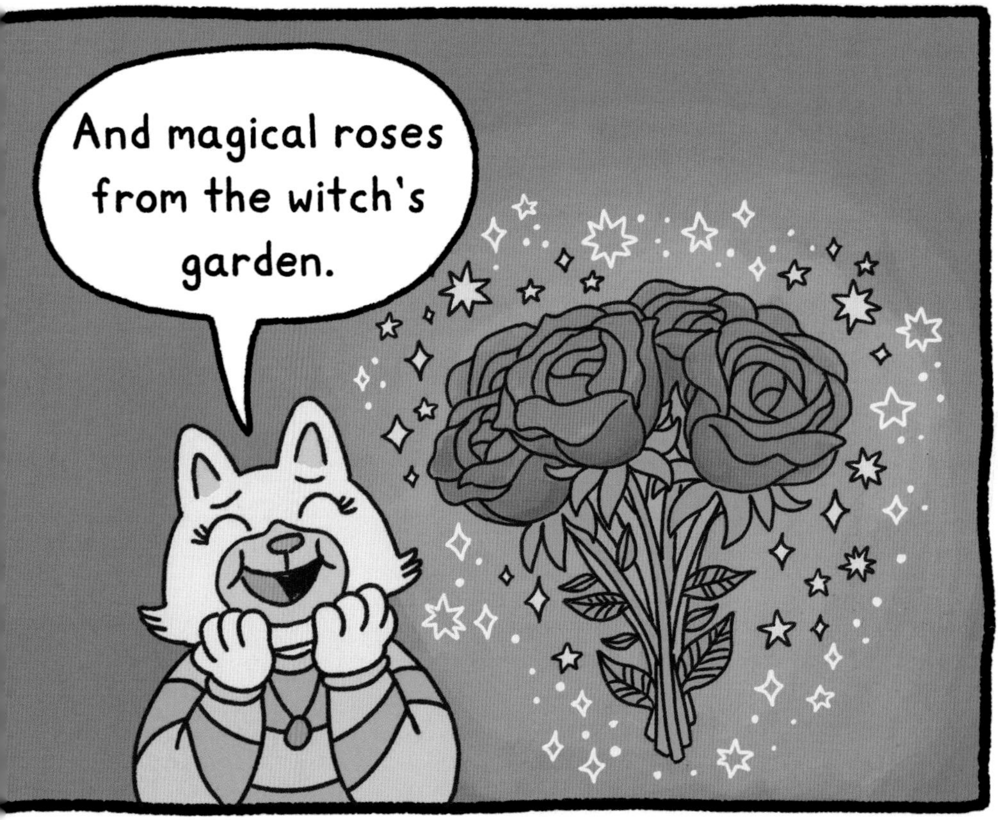
And magical roses from the witch's garden.

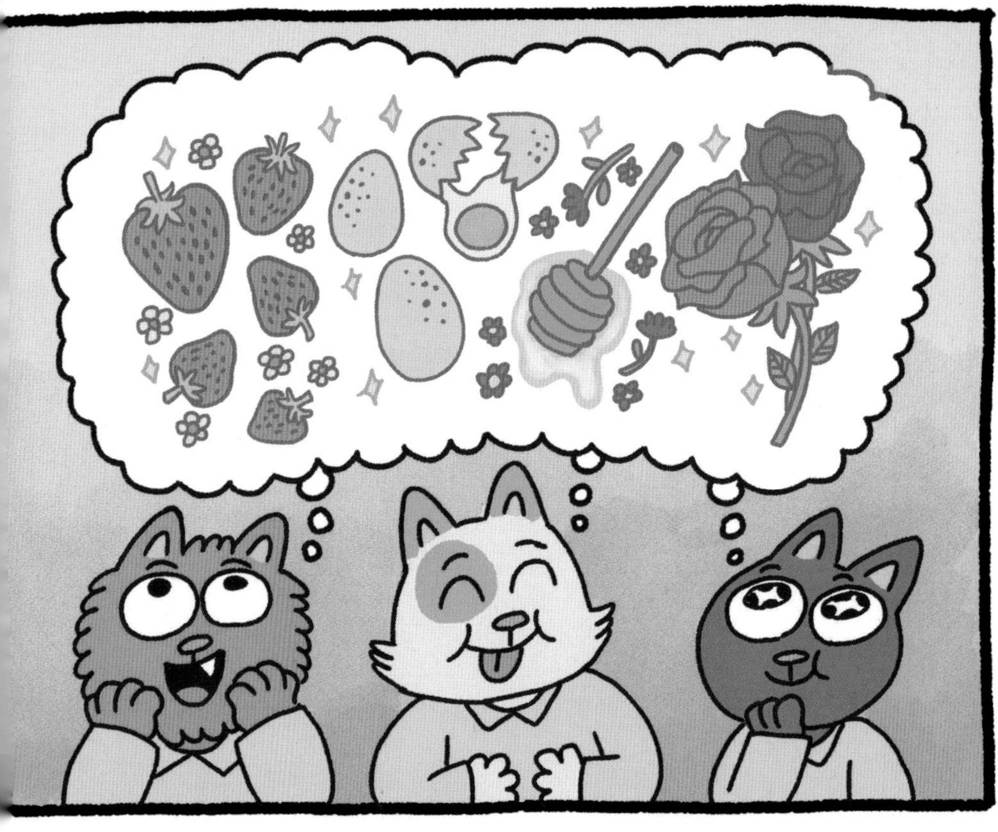

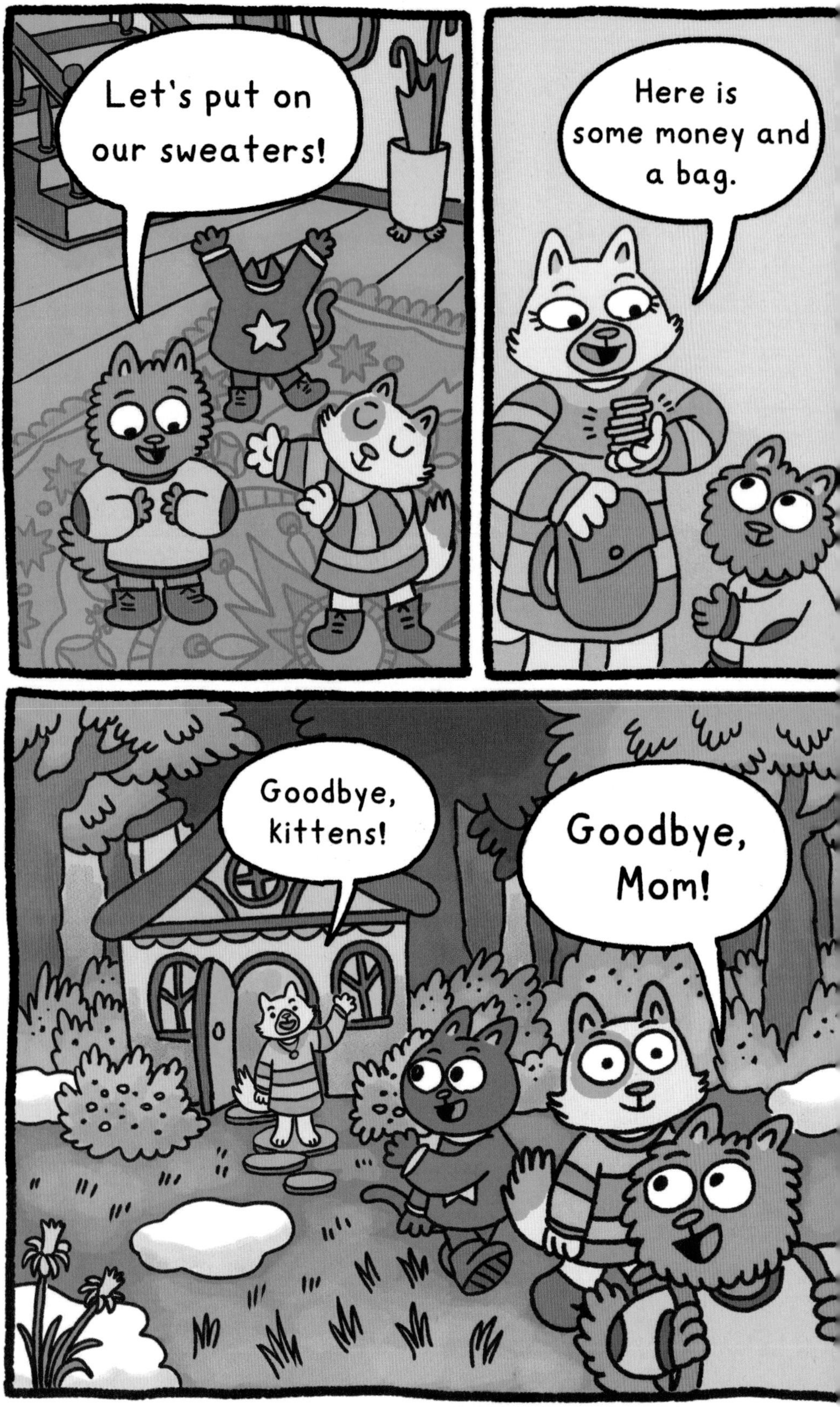
Let's put on our sweaters!
Here is some money and a bag.
Goodbye, kittens!
Goodbye, Mom!

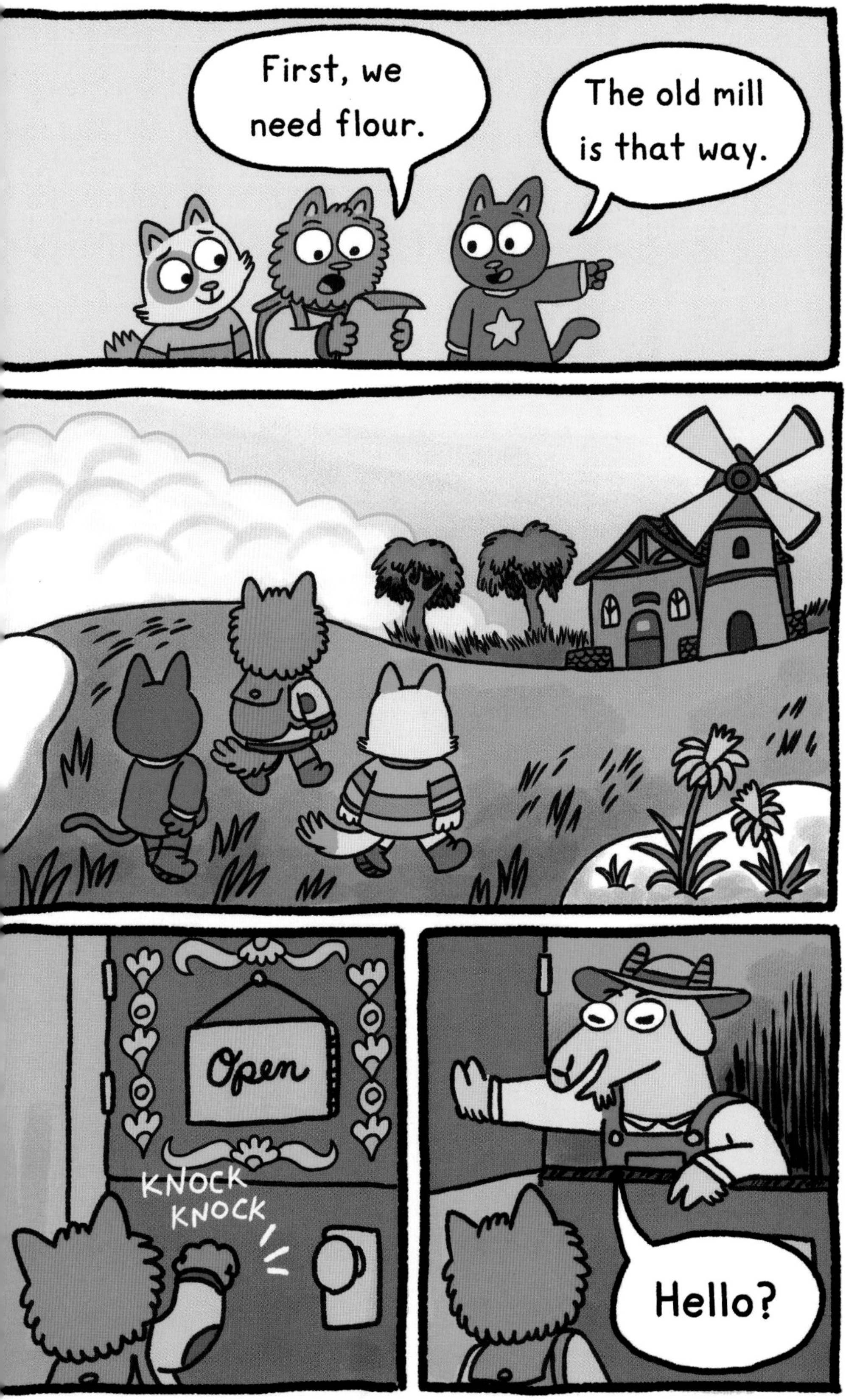

First, we need flour.
The old mill is that way.
Open
KNOCK KNOCK
Hello?

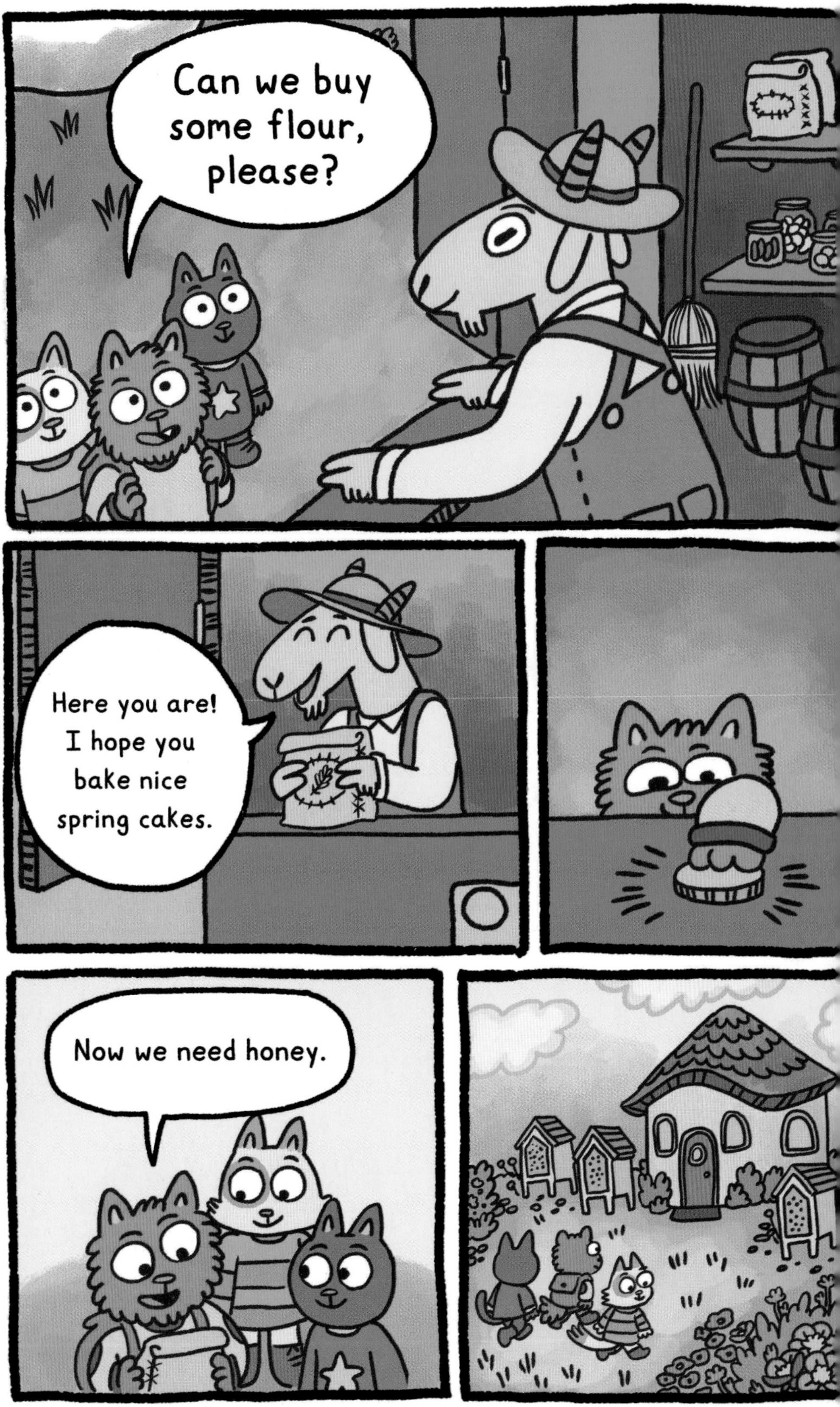
Can we buy some flour, please?
Here you are! I hope you bake nice spring cakes.
Now we need honey.

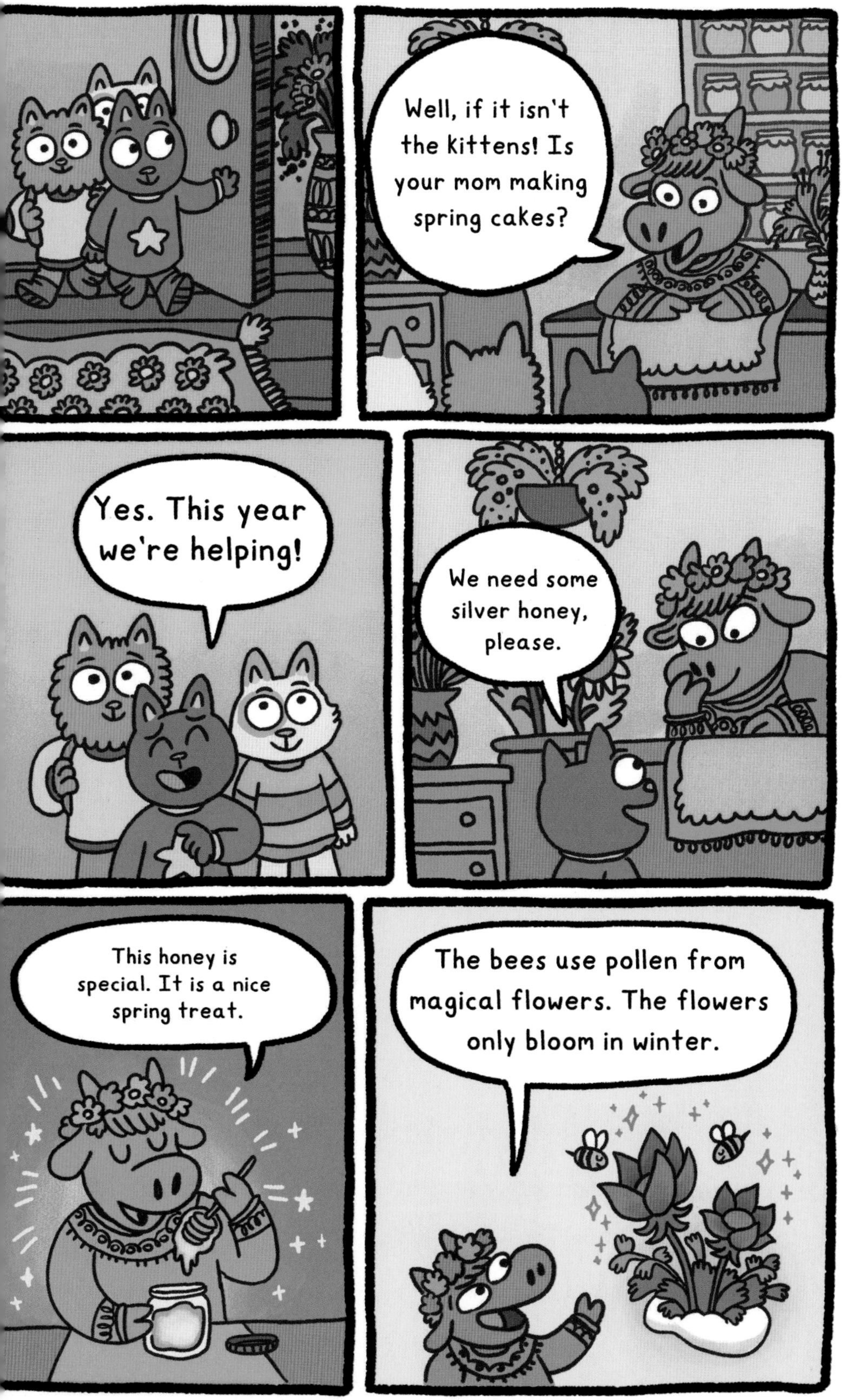
Well, if it isn't the kittens! Is your mom making spring cakes?
Yes. This year we're helping!
We need some silver honey, please.
This honey is special. It is a nice spring treat.
The bees use pollen from magical flowers. The flowers only bloom in winter.

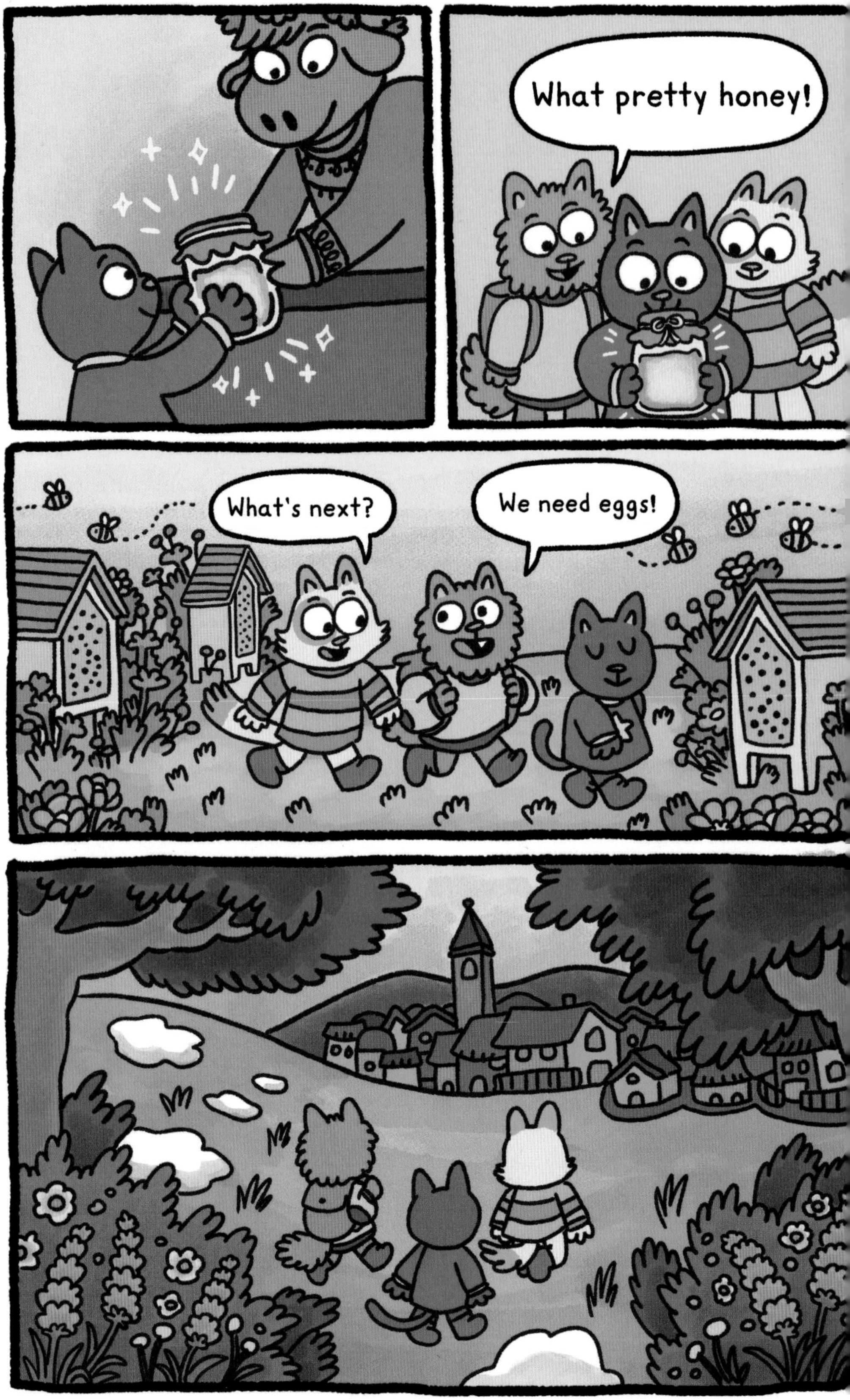
What pretty honey!
What's next?
We need eggs!

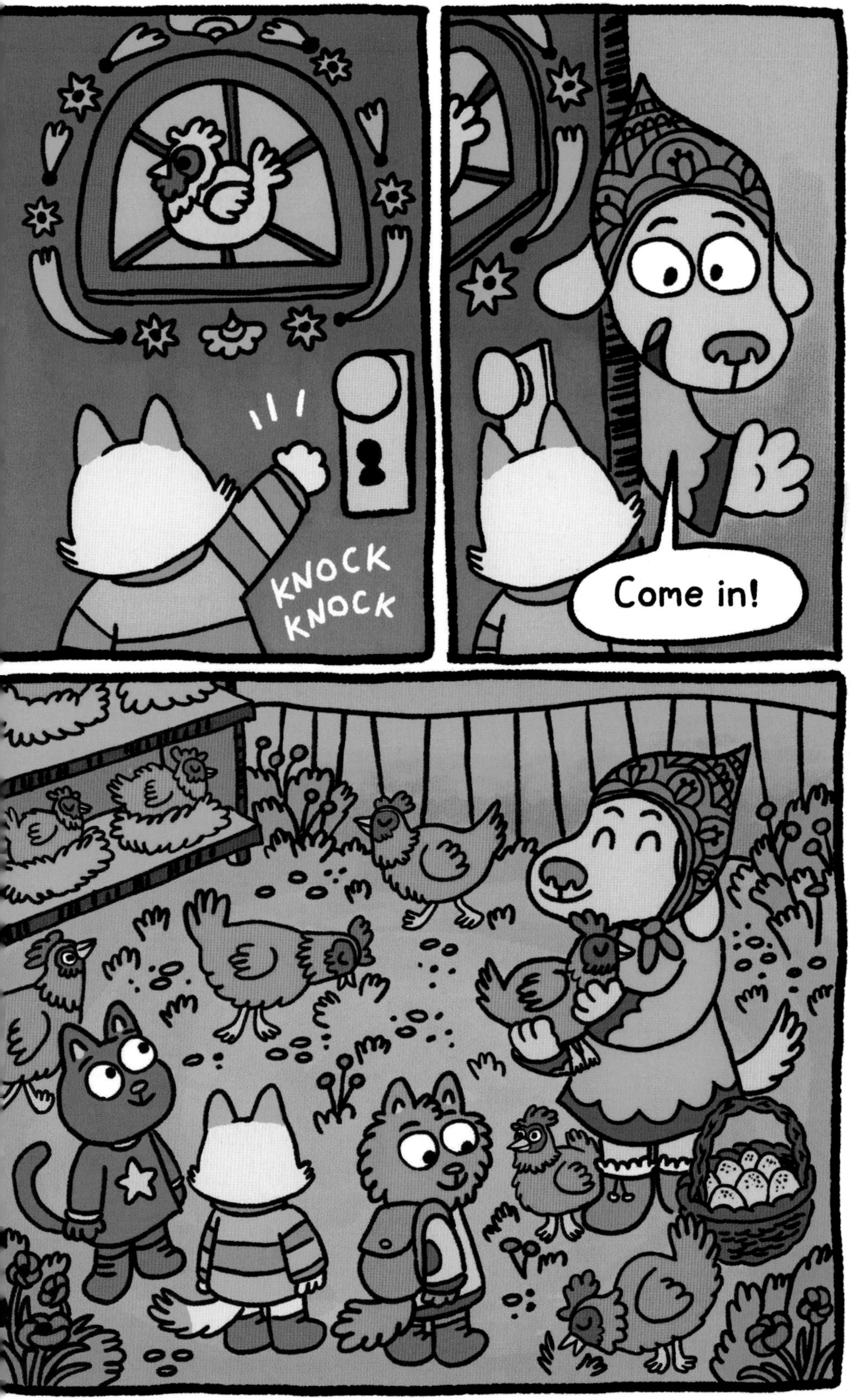
KNOCK
KNOCK
Come in!

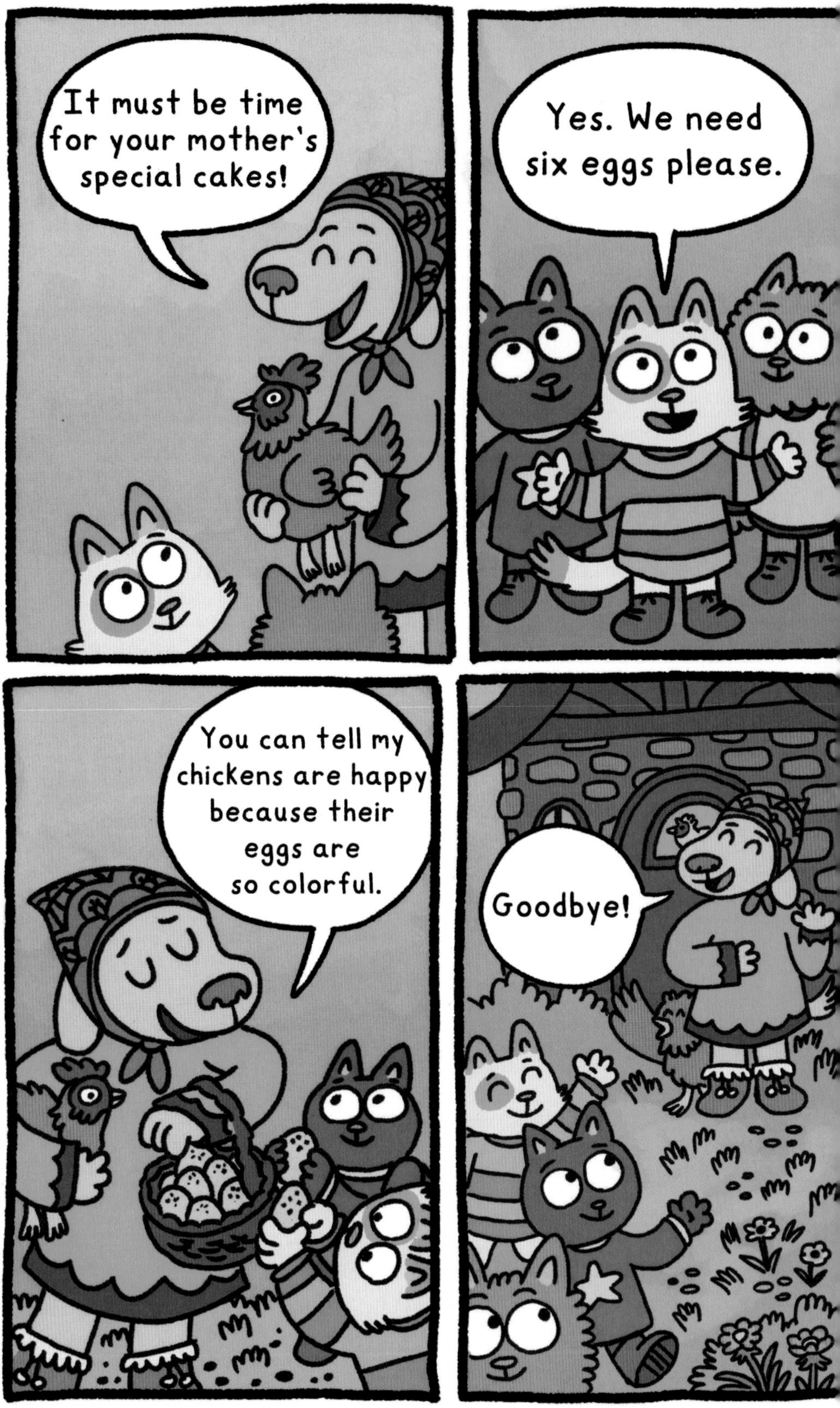
It must be time for your mother's special cakes!
Yes. We need six eggs please.
You can tell my chickens are happy because their eggs are so colorful.
Goodbye!

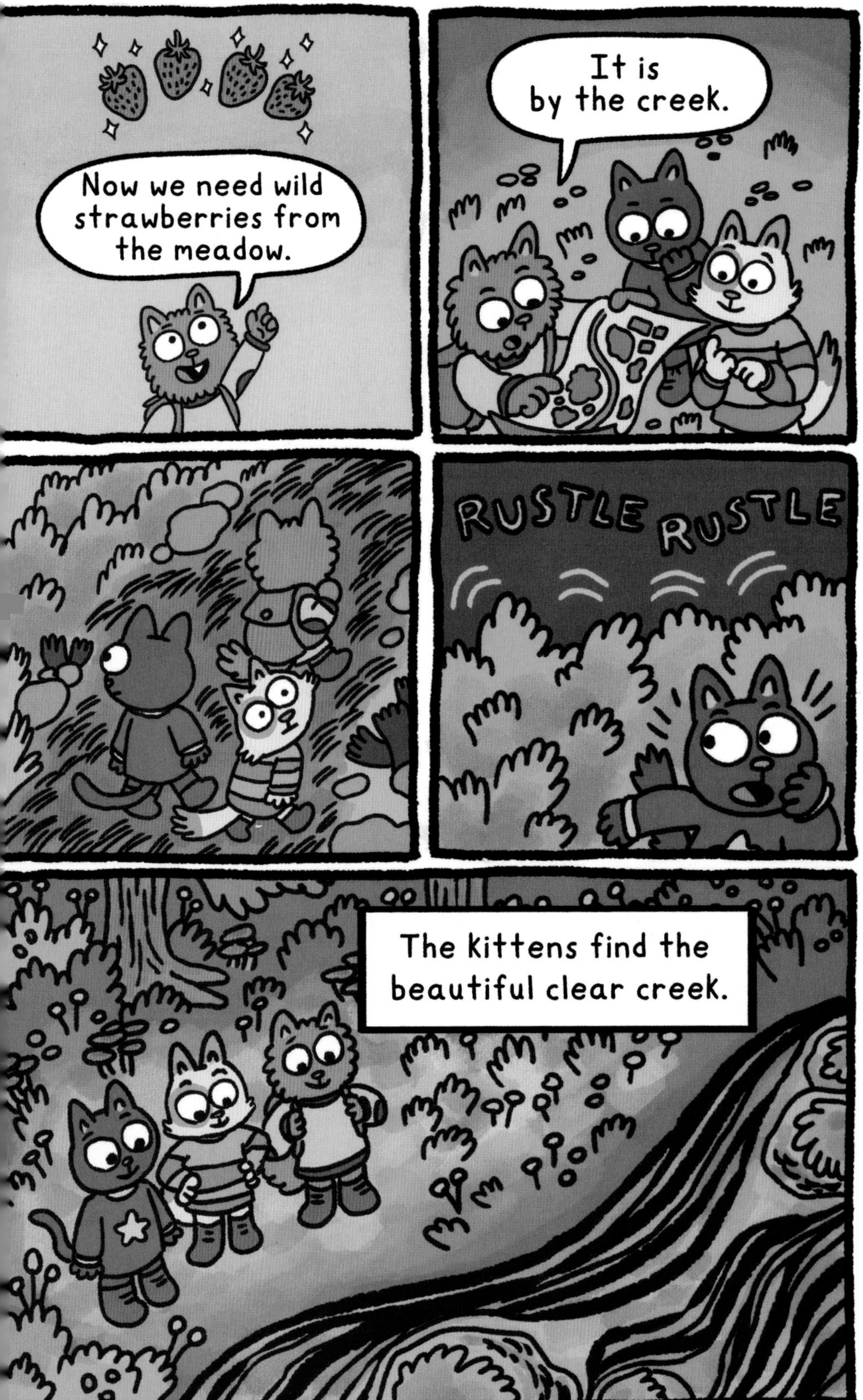
Now we need wild strawberries from the meadow.
It is by the creek.
RUSTLE RUSTLE
The kittens find the beautiful clear creek.

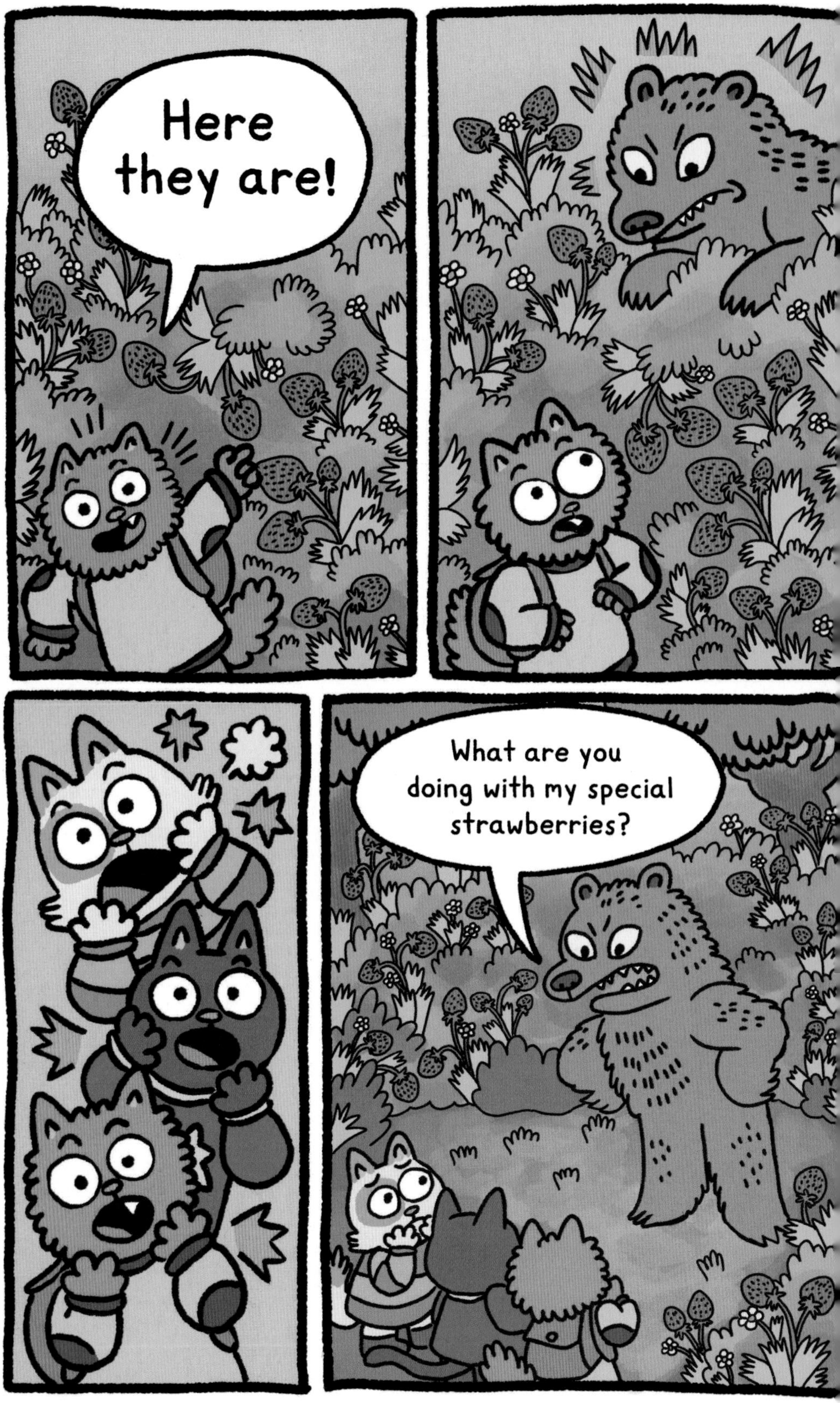
Here they are!
What are you doing with my special strawberries?

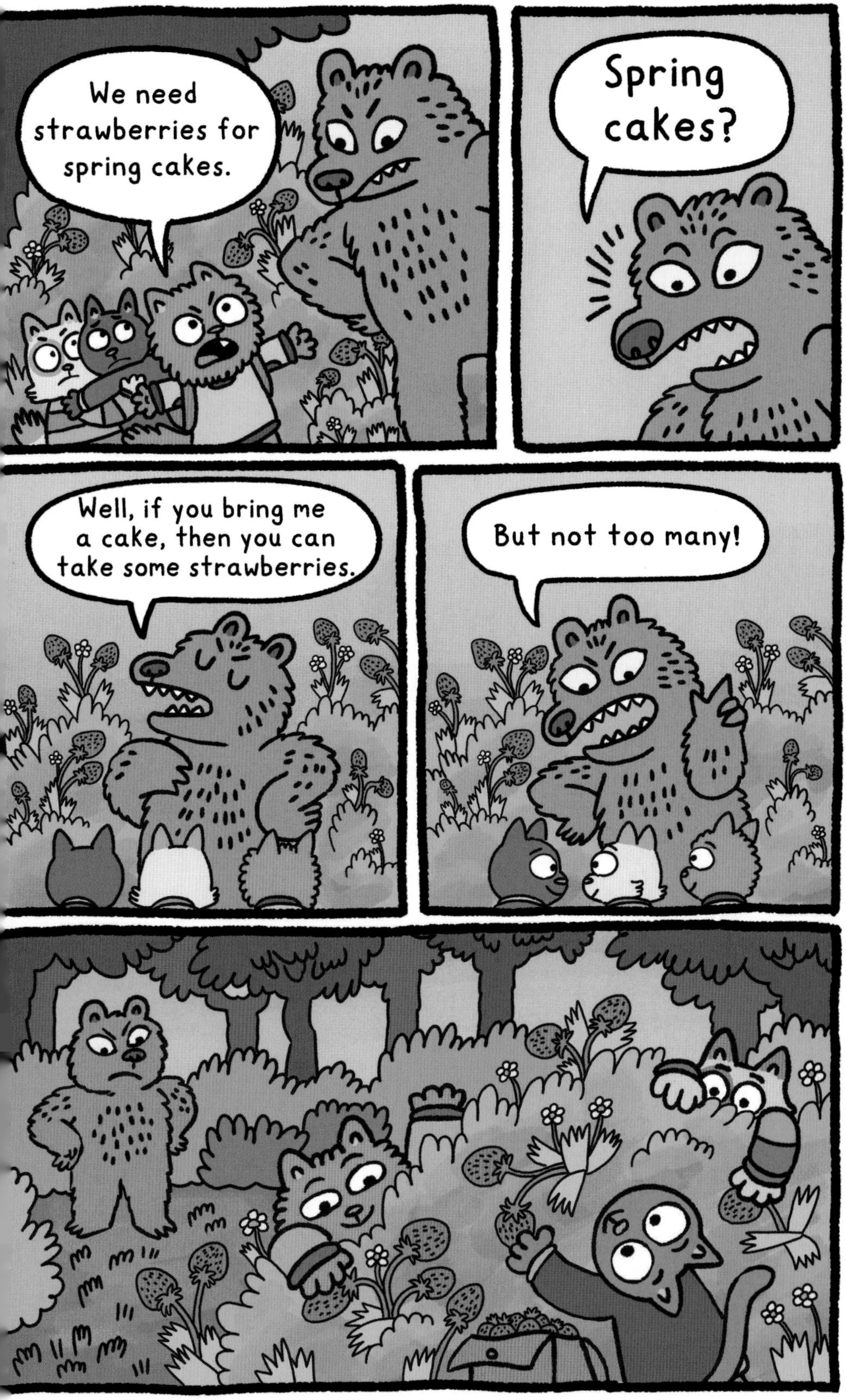
We need strawberries for spring cakes.
Spring cakes?
Well, if you bring me a cake, then you can take some strawberries.
But not too many!

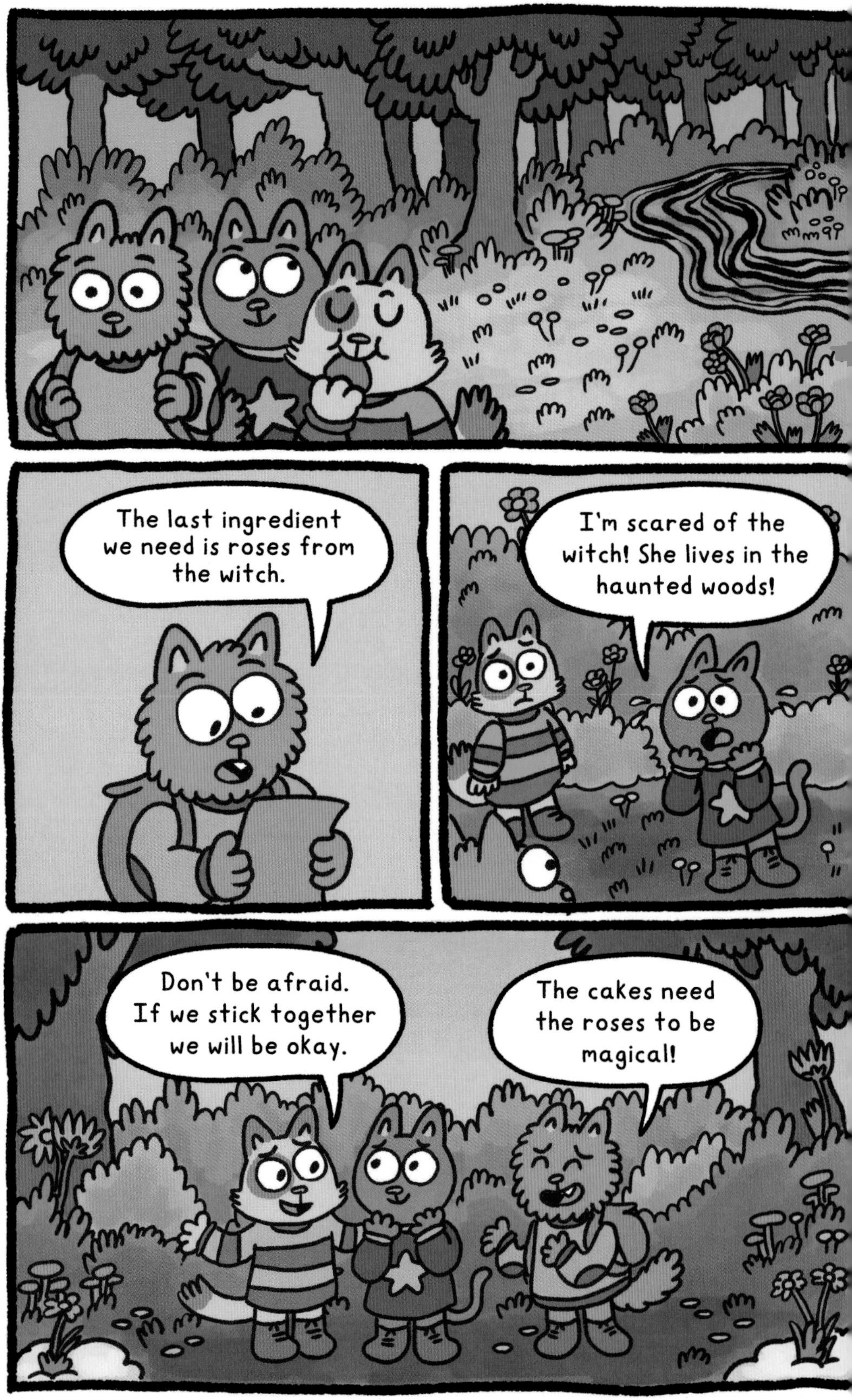
The last ingredient we need is roses from the witch.
I'm scared of the witch! She lives in the haunted woods!
Don't be afraid. If we stick together we will be okay.
The cakes need the roses to be magical!

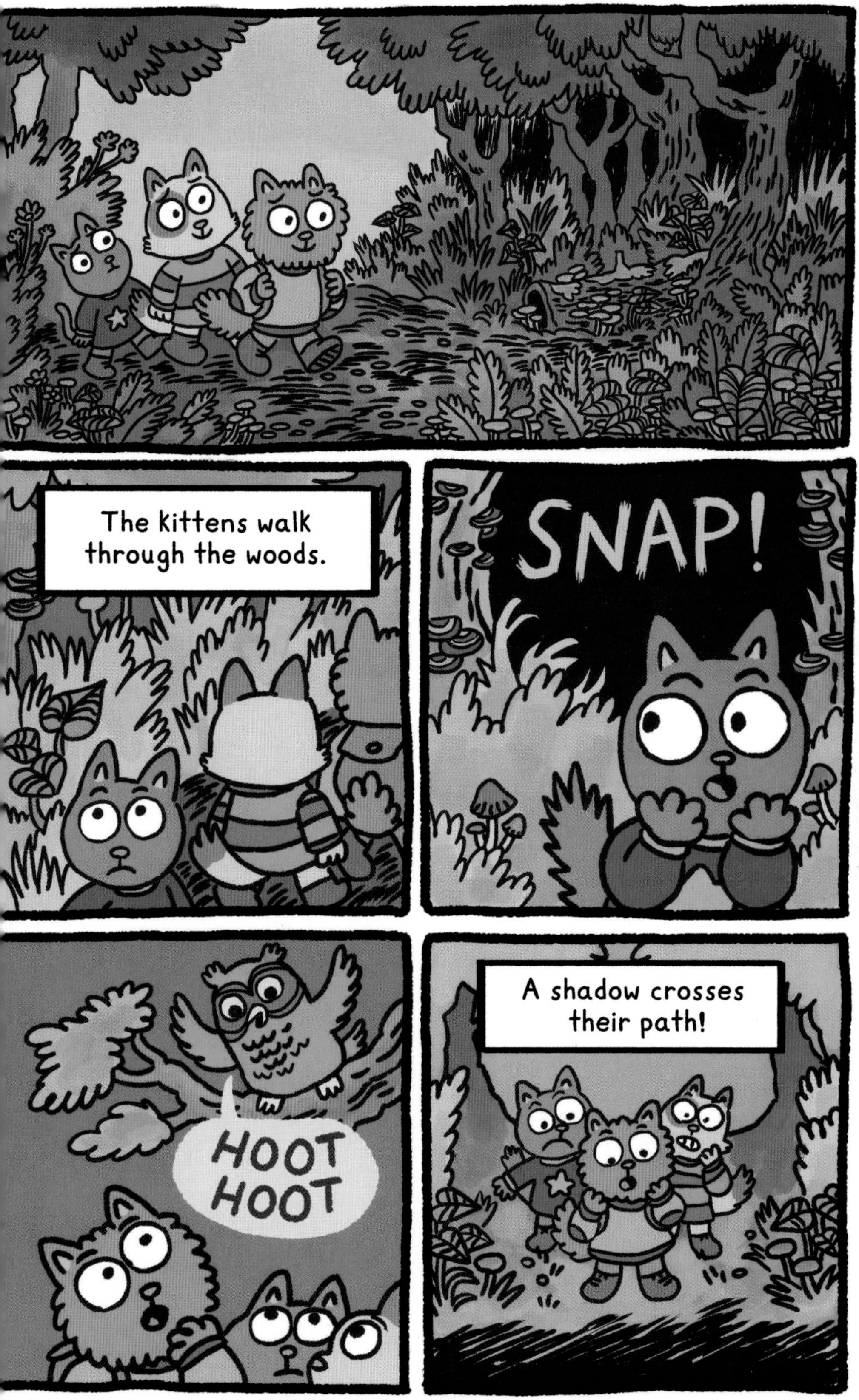
The kittens walk through the woods.
SNAP!
HOOT HOOT
A shadow crosses their path!

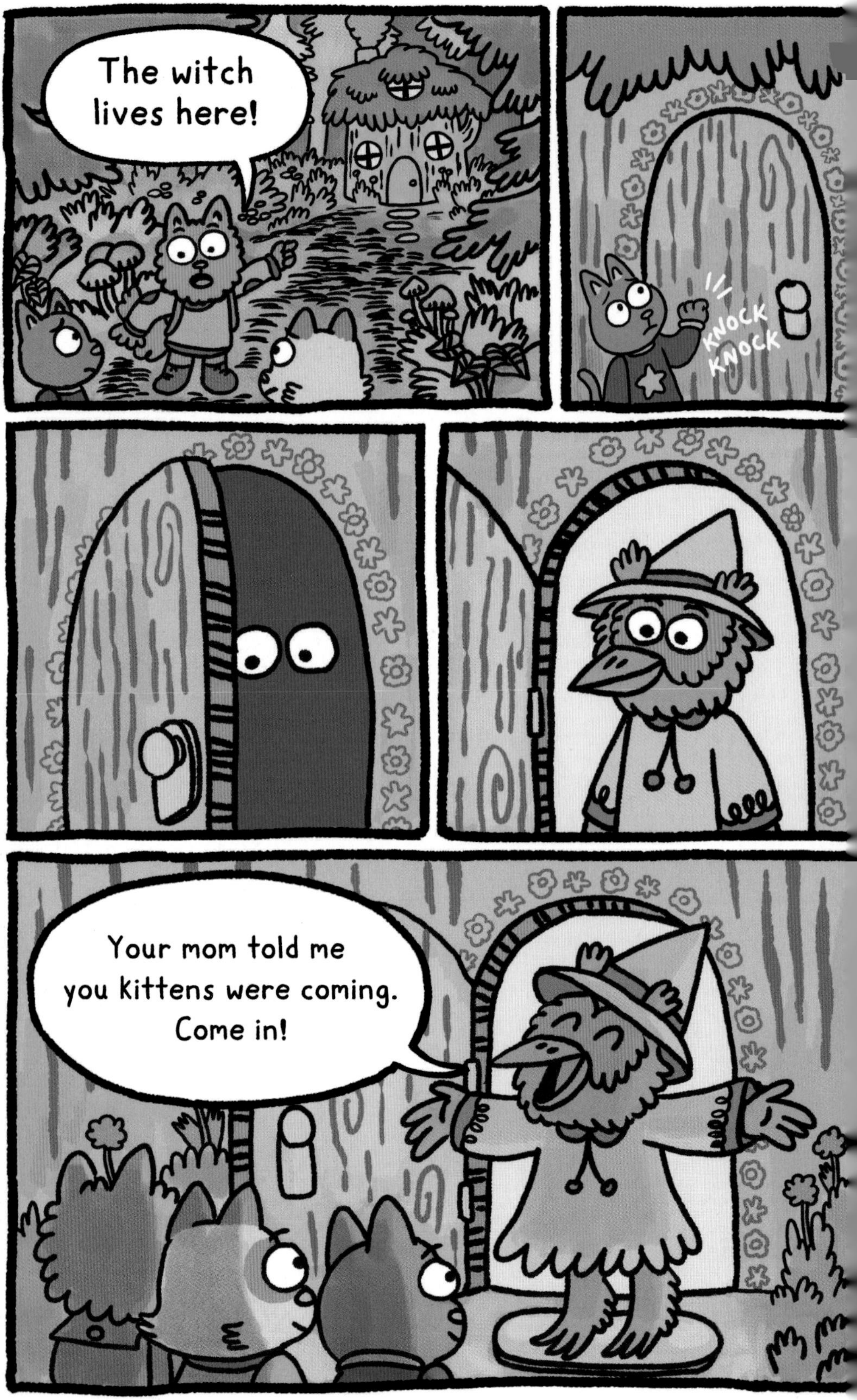
The witch lives here!
KNOCK KNOCK
Your mom told me you kittens were coming. Come in!

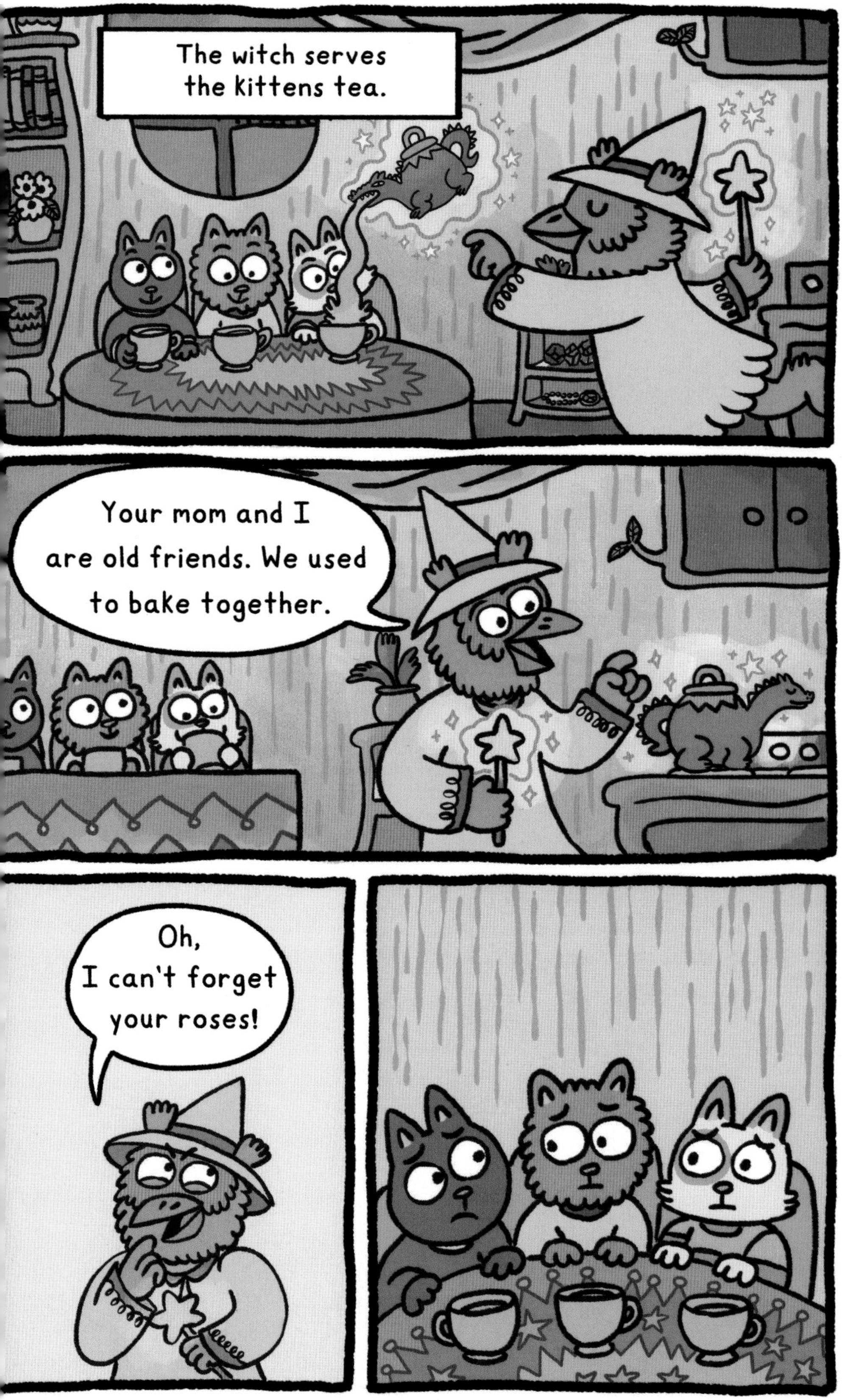
The witch serves the kittens tea.
Your mom and I are old friends. We used to bake together.
Oh, I can't forget your roses!

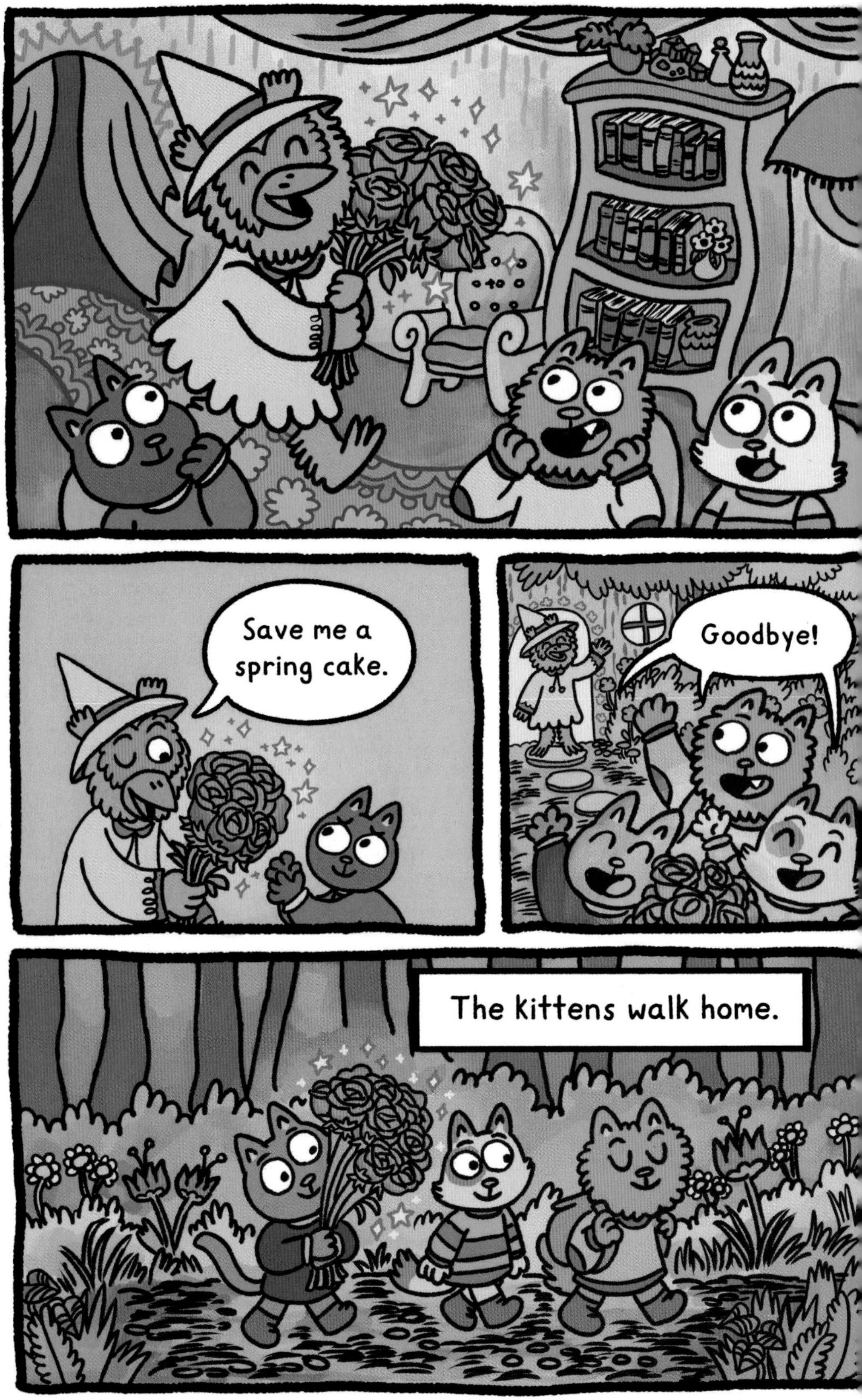
Save me a spring cake.
Goodbye!
The kittens walk home.

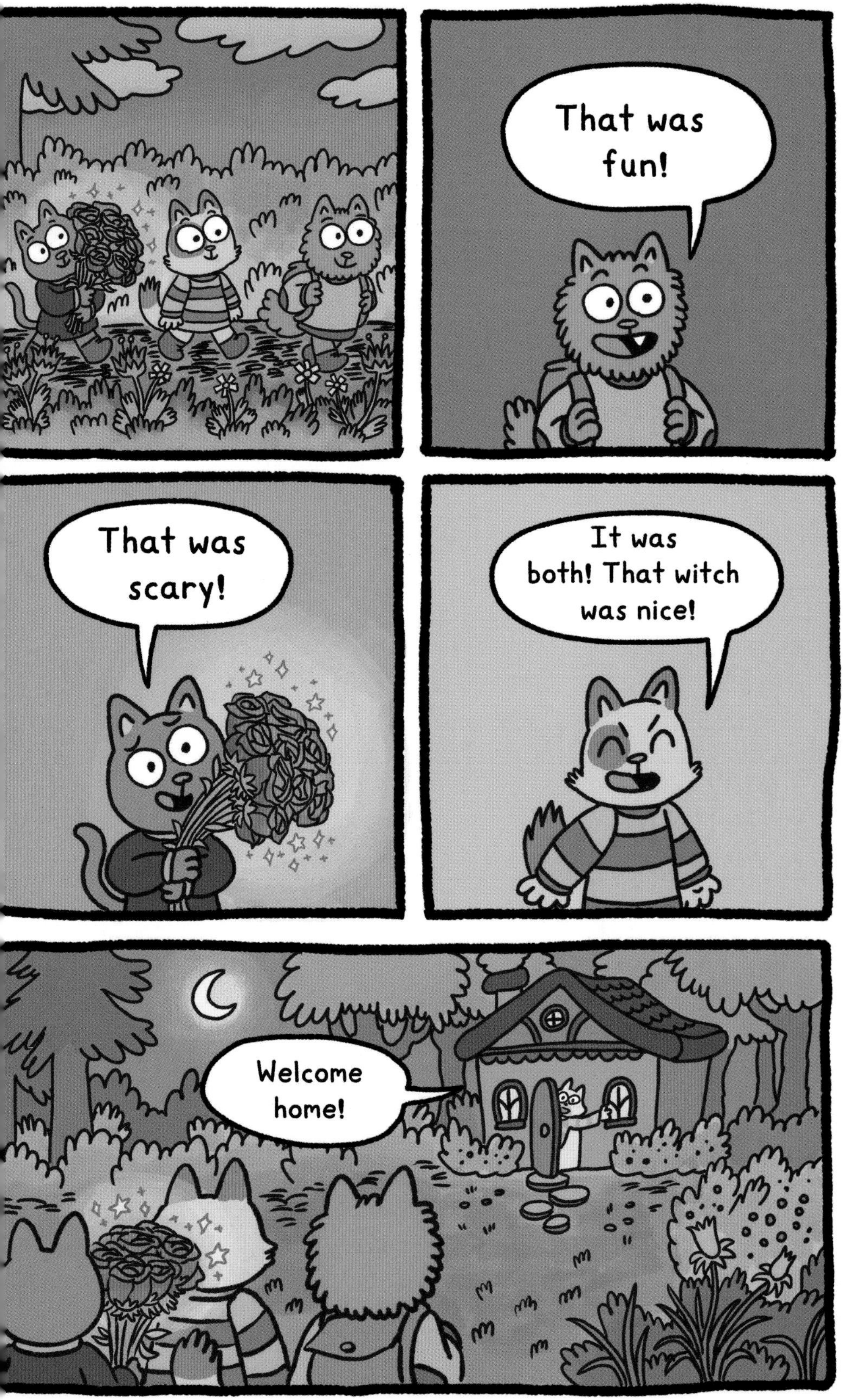
That was fun!
That was scary!
It was both! That witch was nice!
Welcome home!

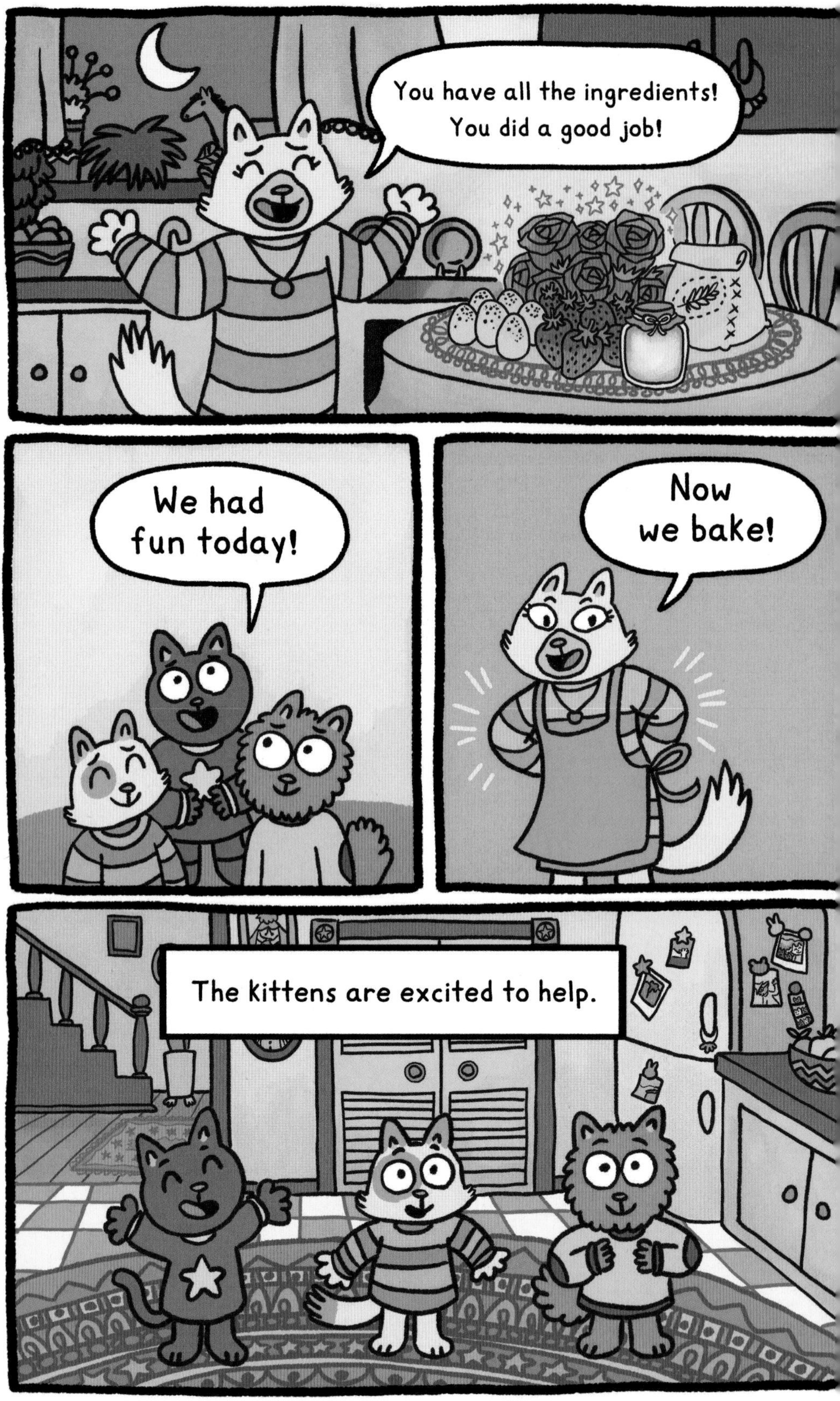
You have all the ingredients! You did a good job!
We had fun today!
Now we bake!
The kittens are excited to help.

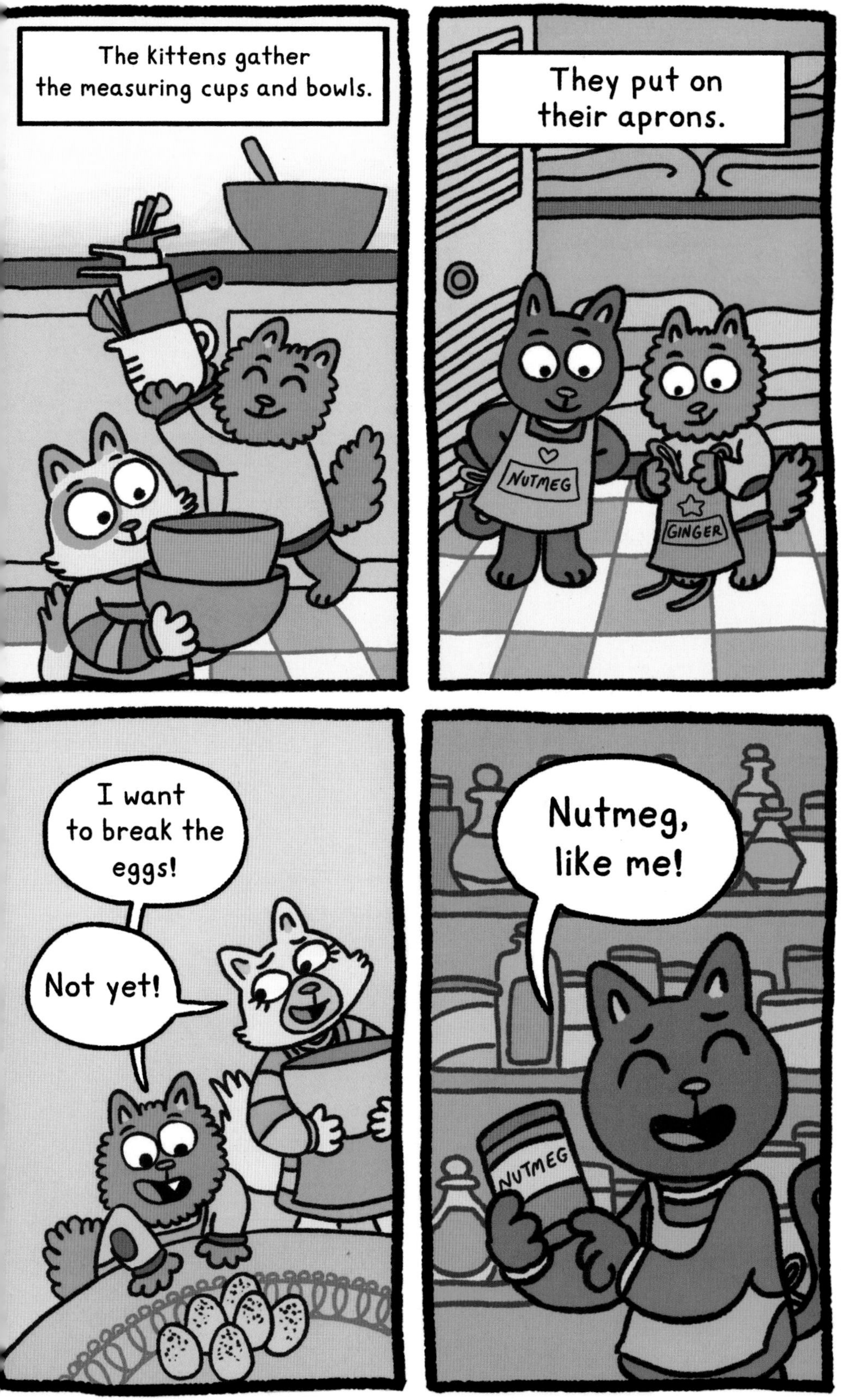
The kittens gather the measuring cups and bowls.
They put on their aprons.
NUTMEG
GINGER
I want to break the eggs!
Not yet!
Nutmeg, like me!
NUTMEG

First we mix the dry ingredients.
Cinnamon measures the flour. Nutmeg measures the baking powder.
Ginger measures out spices and puts them in.
Mom puts in the sugar.
Can I break the eggs yet?
No, not yet, Ginger!

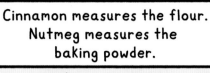

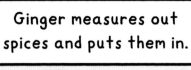

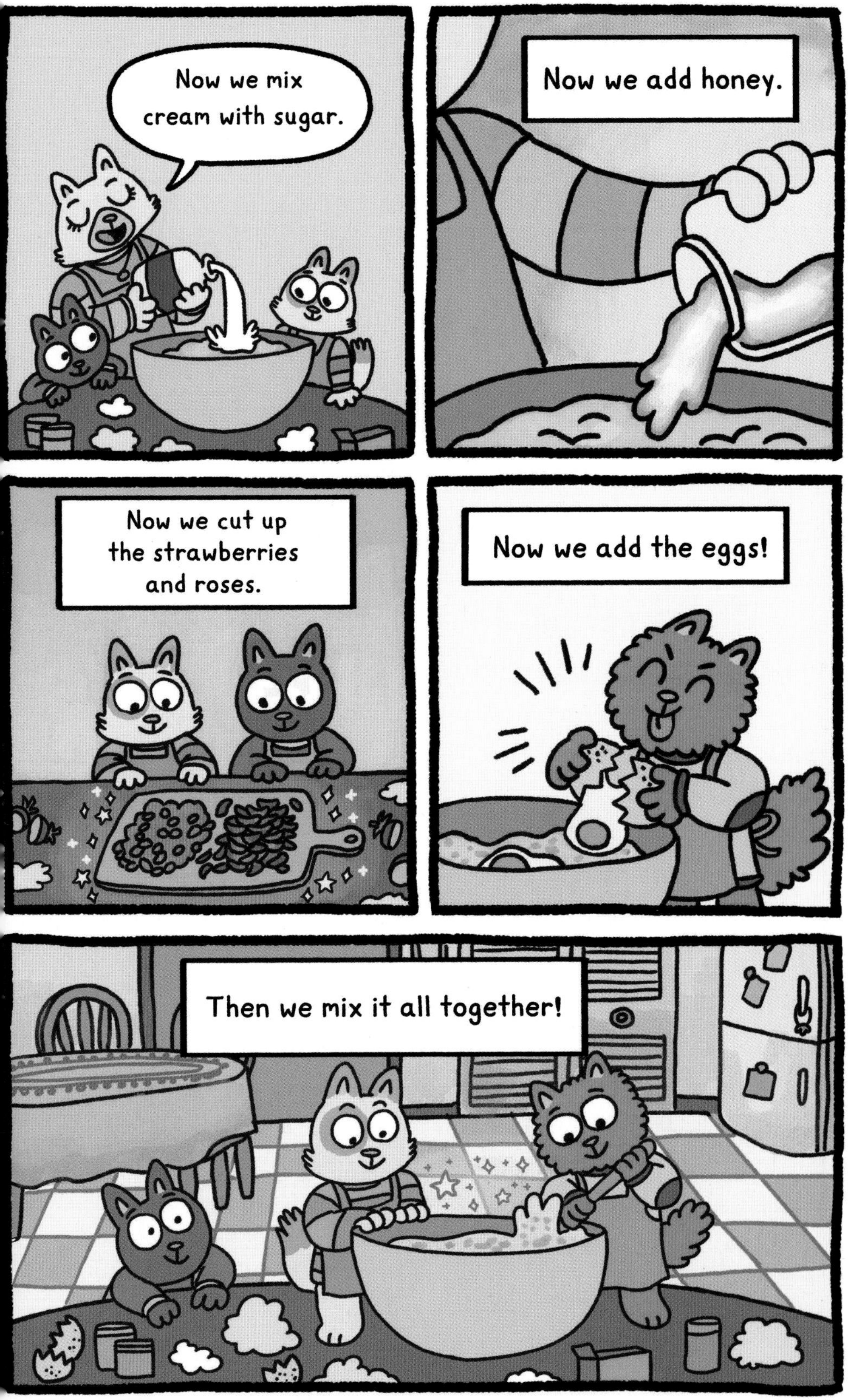
Now we mix
cream with sugar.
Now we add honey.
Now we cut up
the strawberries
and roses.
Now we add the eggs!
Then we mix it all together!

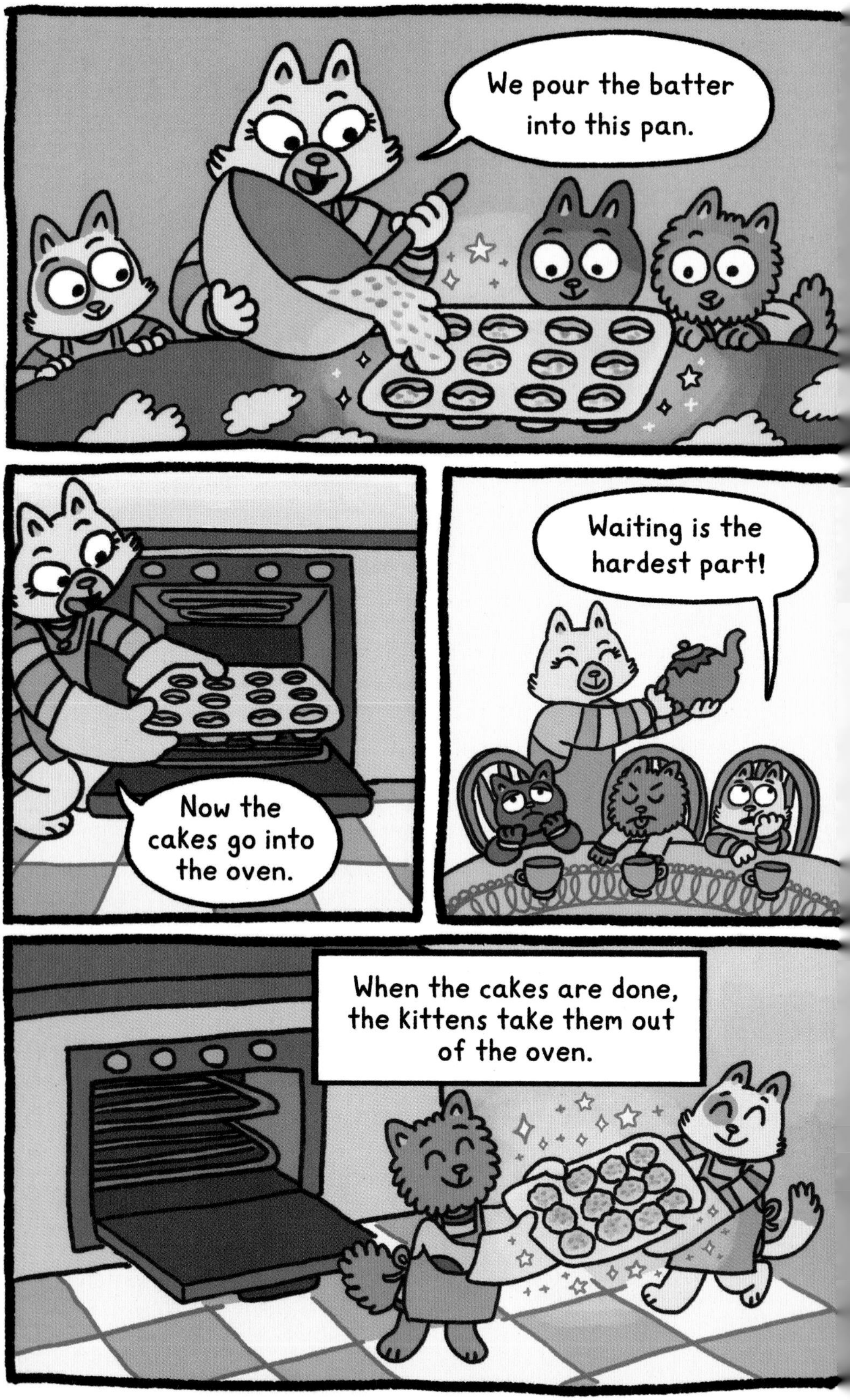
We pour the batter into this pan.
Now the cakes go into the oven.
Waiting is the hardest part!
When the cakes are done, the kittens take them out of the oven.

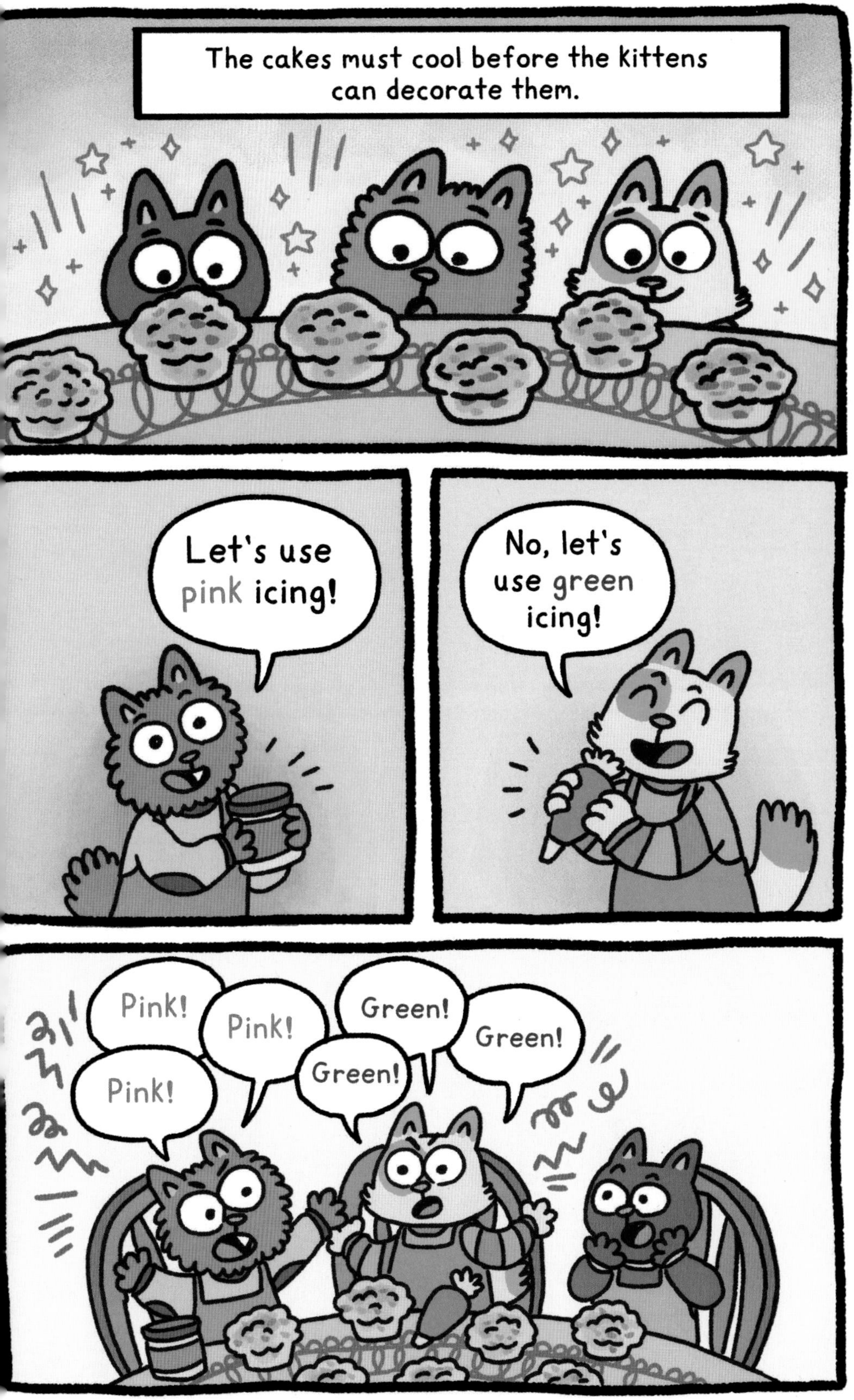
The cakes must cool before the kittens can decorate them.
Let's use pink icing!
No, let's use green icing!
Pink!
Pink!
Pink!
Green!
Green!
Green!

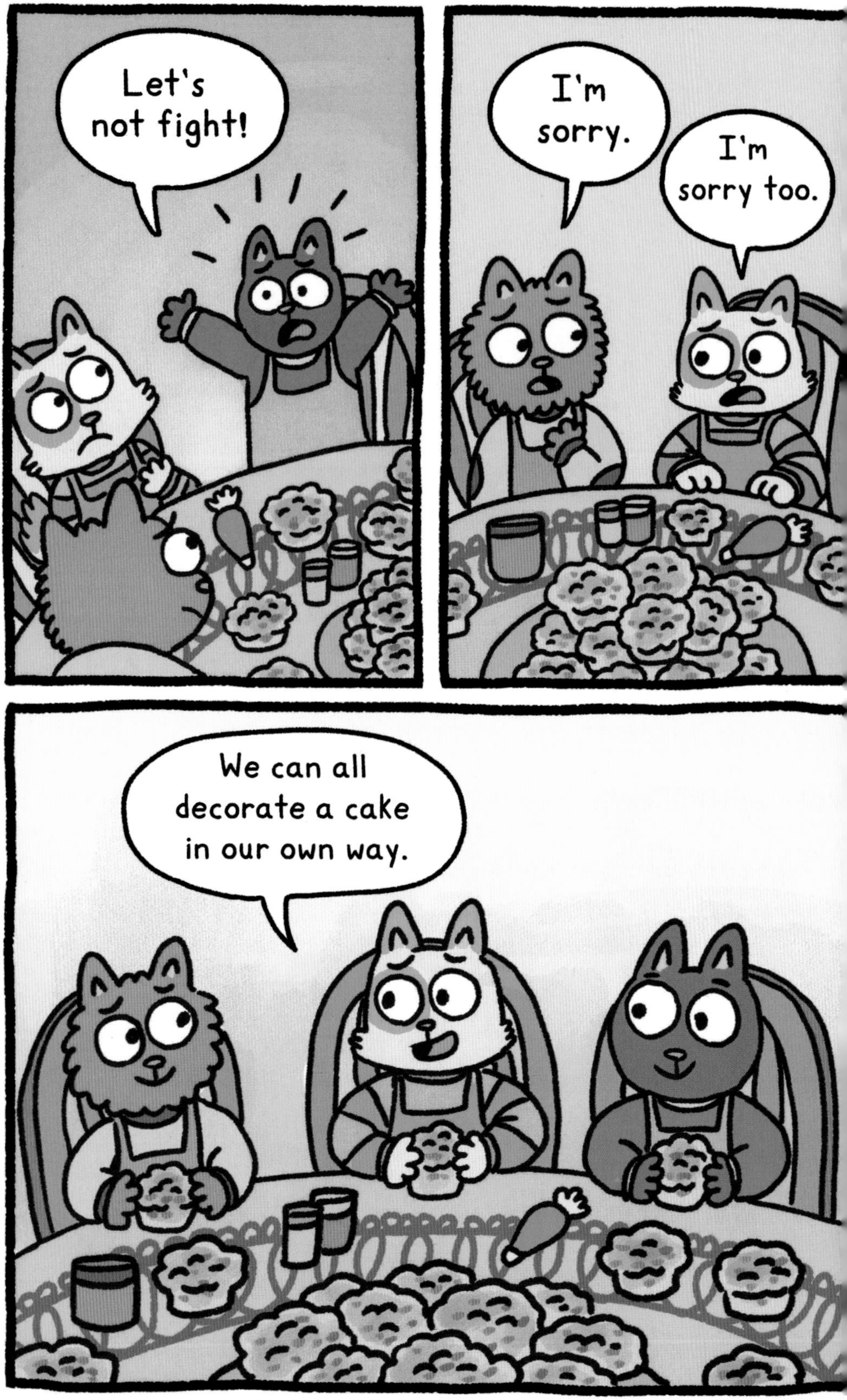
Let's not fight!
I'm sorry.
I'm sorry too.
We can all decorate a cake in our own way.

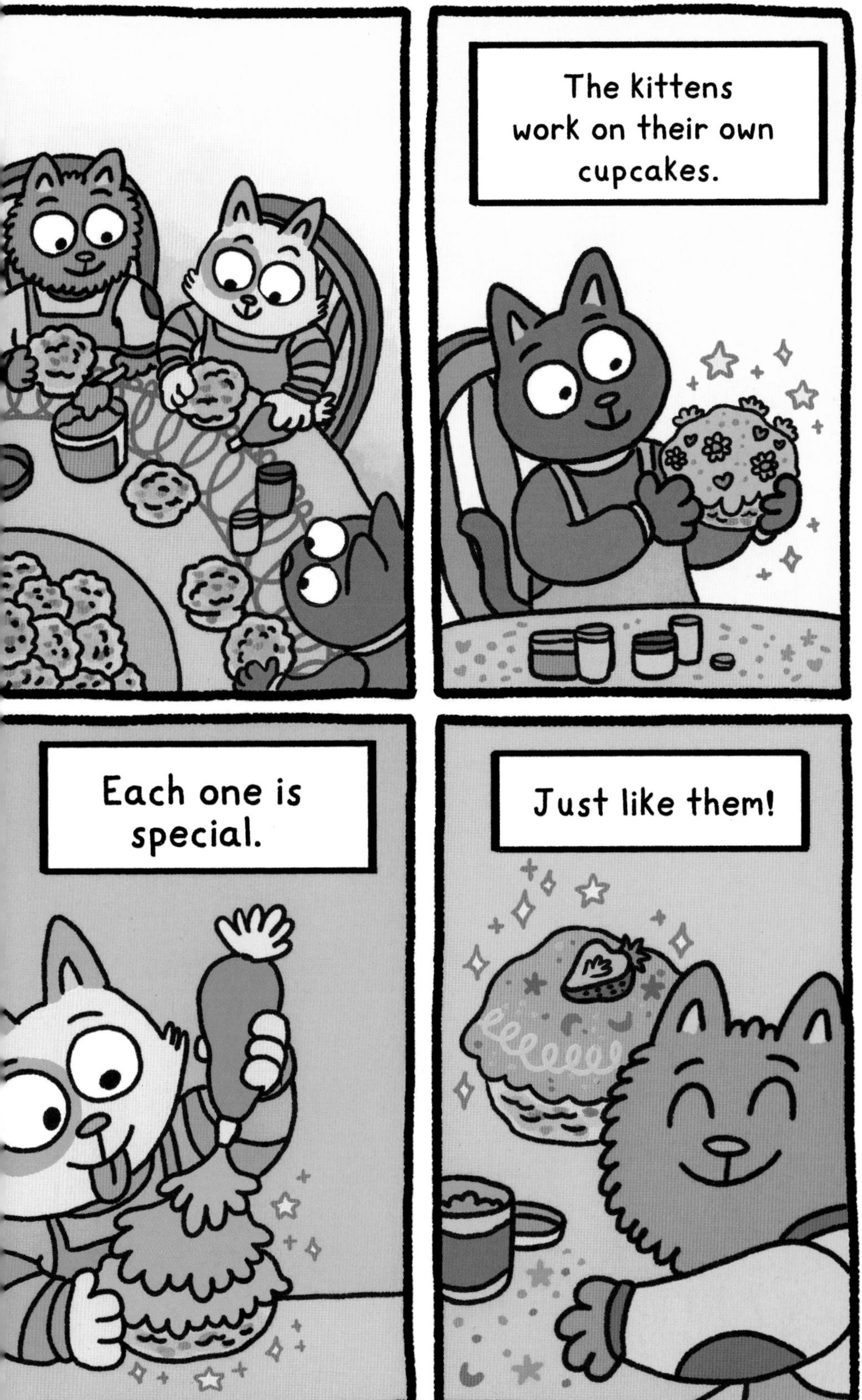
The kittens work on their own cupcakes.
Each one is special.
Just like them!

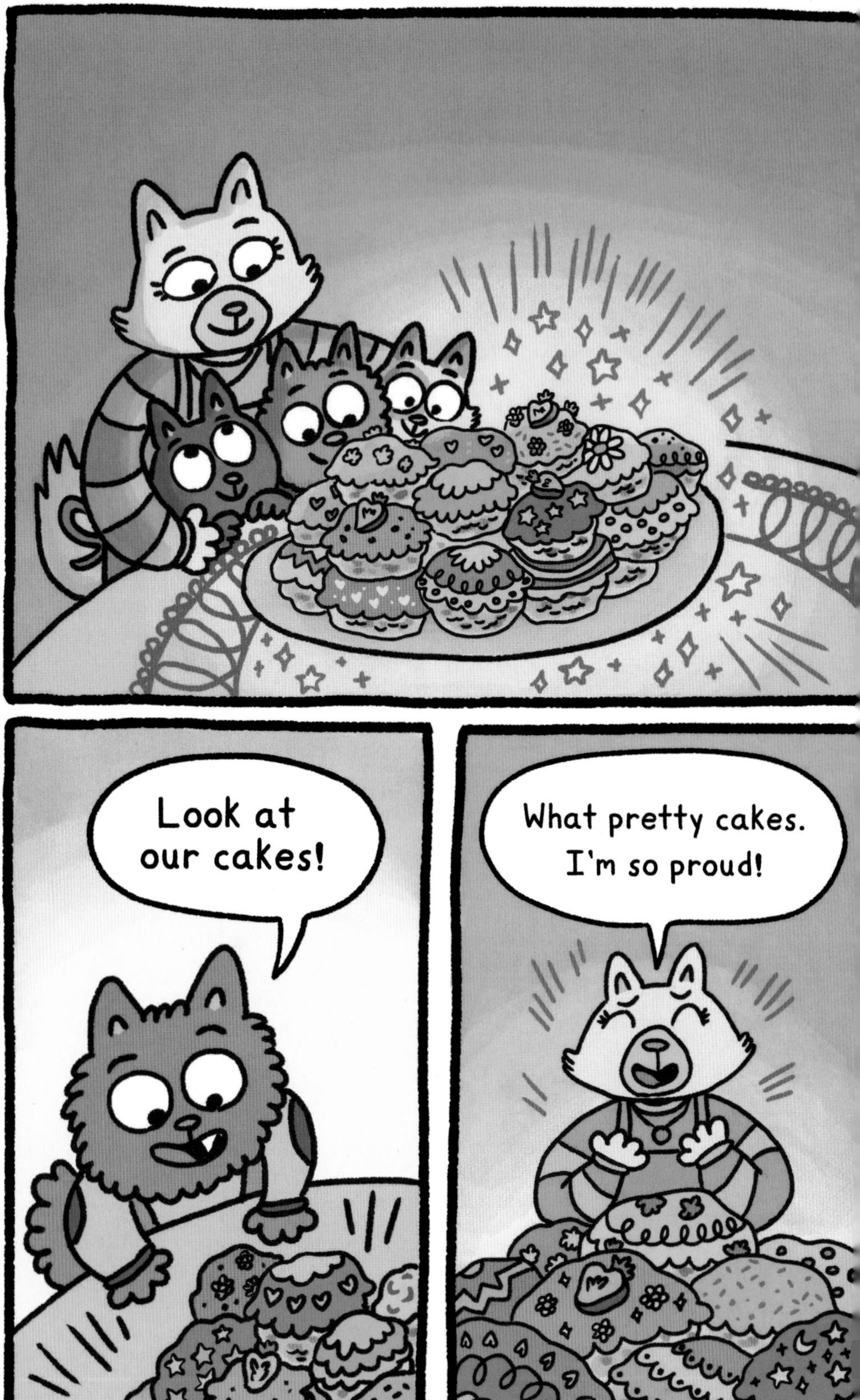

Look at our cakes!
What pretty cakes. I'm so proud!

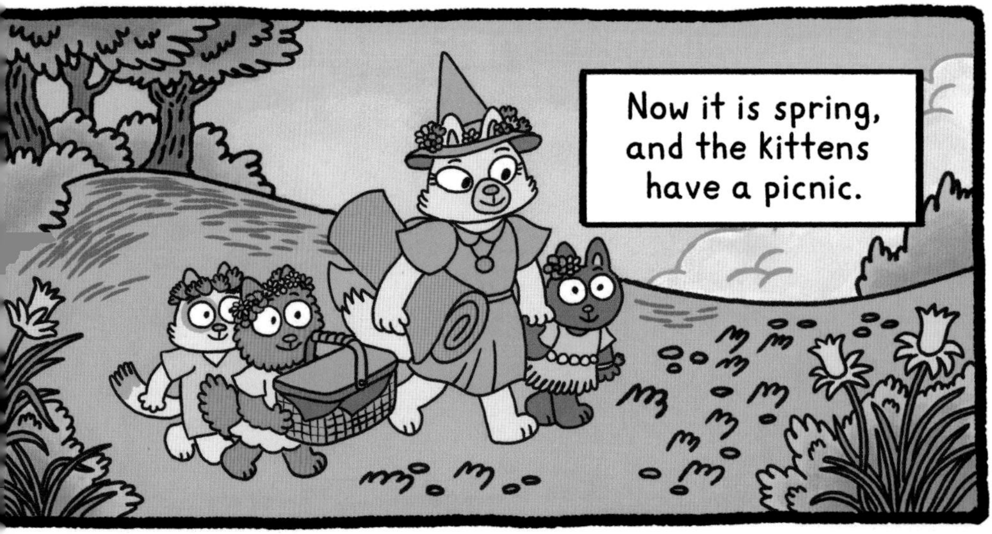
Now it is spring, and the kittens have a picnic.

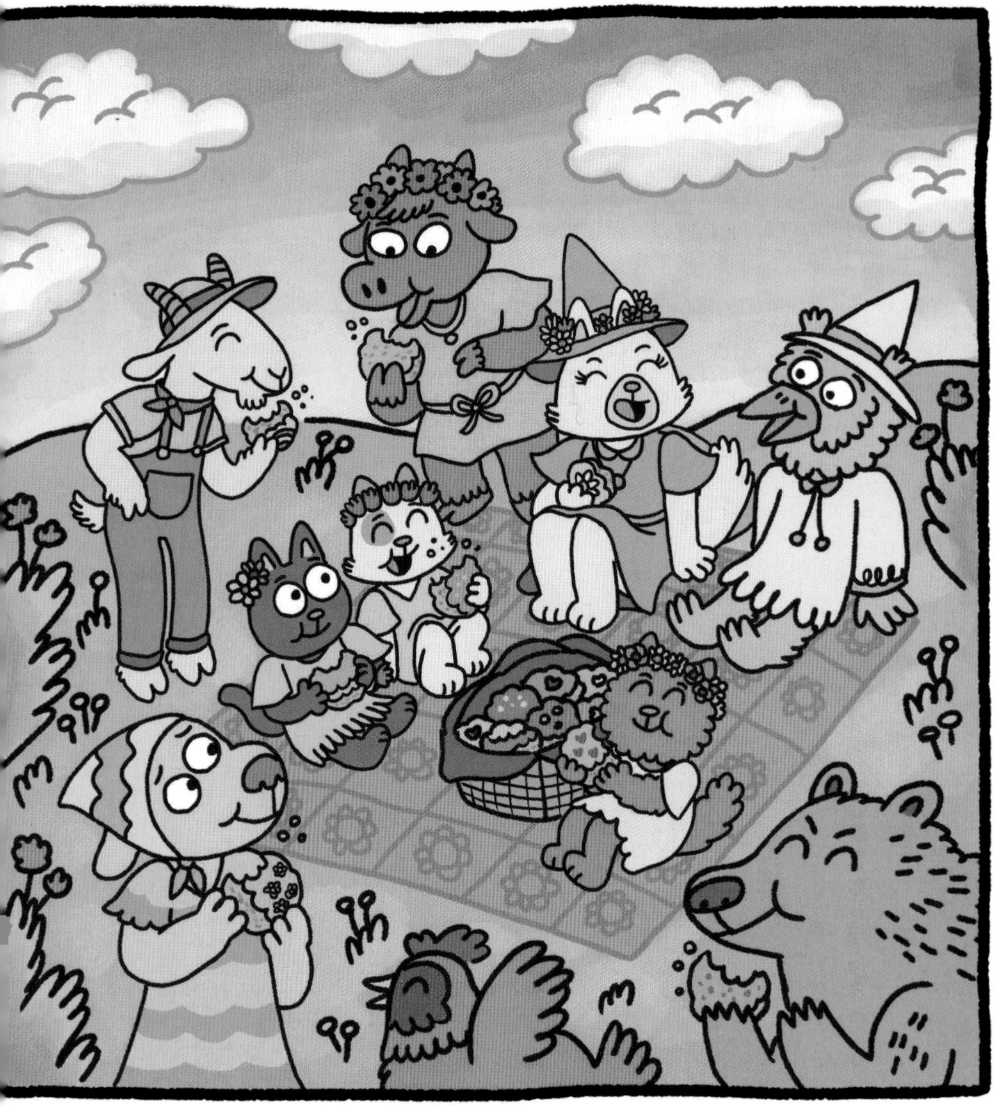

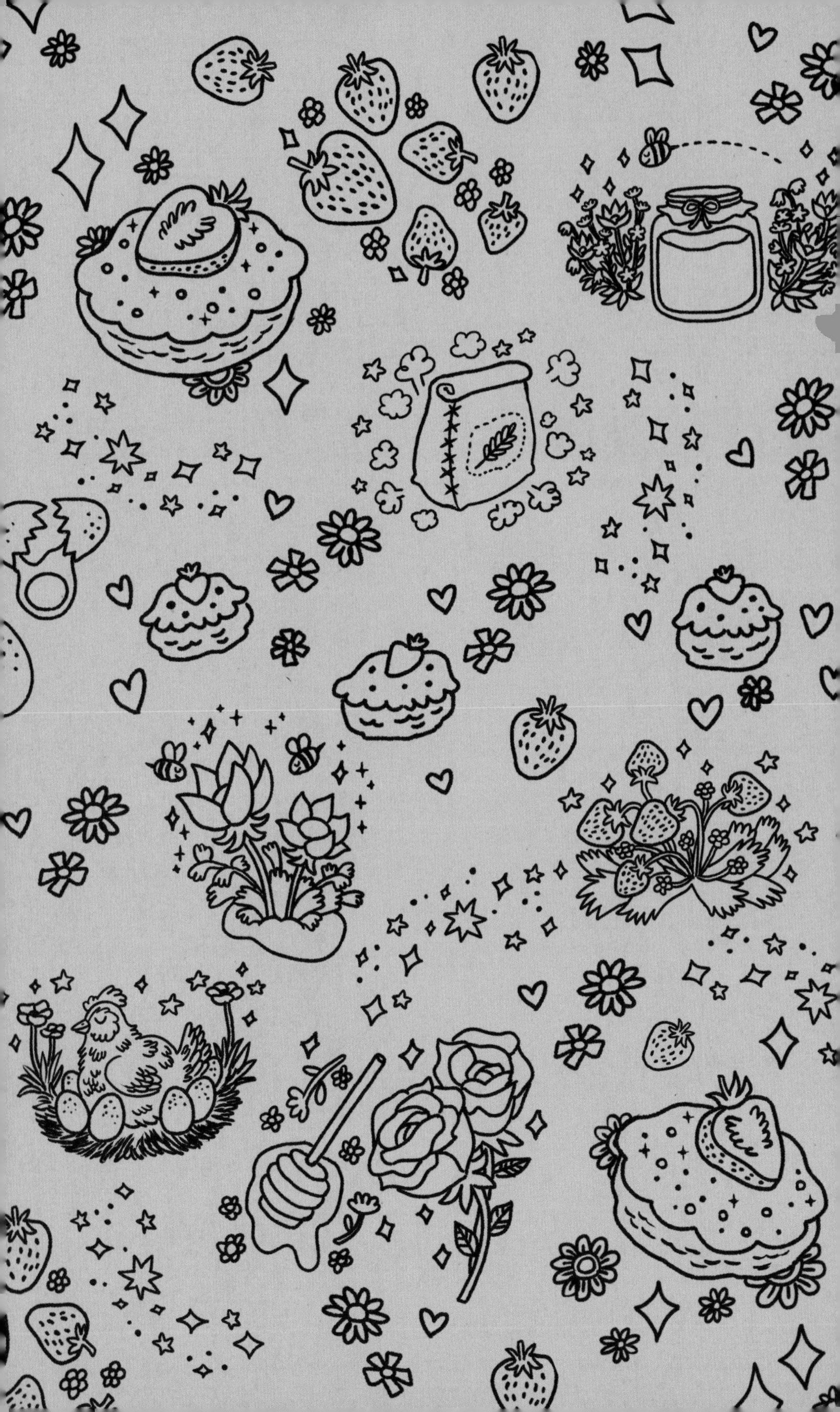